STRAWBERRY DRAGON

FAIRCHILD, VOLUME TWO

BLAZE WARD

KNOTTED ROAD PRESS

Strawberry Dragon
Fairchild, Volume Two
Copyright © 2021 Blaze Ward
All rights reserved
Published by Knotted Road Press
www.KnottedRoadPress.com

ISBN: 78-1-64470-255-0

Cover art:
Illustration 174113584 © Vgorbash | Dreamstime.com

Cover and interior design copyright © 2021 Knotted Road Press

Reviews
It's true. Reviews help. Even a short one, such as, "Loved it!" So please consider reviewing this book (and all of the ones you've read) on your favorite retailer site.

Never miss a release!
If you'd like to be notified of new releases, sign up for my newsletter.

http://www.blazeward.com/newsletter/

Buy More!
Did you know that you can buy directly from my website?

https://www.blazeward.com/shop/

The Lazarus Alliance

Escape

Return

Rebellion

Revolution

Liberation

Retribution

Alliance

The Jessica Keller Chronicles

Auberon

Queen of the Pirates

Last of the Immortals

Goddess of War

Flight of the Blackbird

The Red Admiral

St. Legier

Winterhome

Petron

CS-405

Queen Anne's Revenge

Packmule

Persephone

Additional Alexandria Station Stories

Siren

Two Bottles of Wine with a War God

The Story Road

The Science Officer Series Season One

The Science Officer

The Mind Field

The Gilded Cage

The Pleasure Dome

The Doomsday Vault

The Last Flagship

The Hammerfield Gambit

The Hammerfield Payoff

The Bryce Connection

The Science Officer Series Season Two

Alien Seas

Shadow of the Dominion

Longshot Hypothesis

Hard Bargain

Outermost

Dominion-427

Phoenix

Princess Rualoh

For Allyson

CONTENTS

PART ONE

FIRST CONTACT

CHAPTER ONE

R'WN

THE WIDE GAP between this forest and the next one, that magical thing over there, always gave R'wn pause. Not many dragons were blessed to be present at the birth of a new theology. Mostly, R'wn was just pissed that those invaders had decided to do it in his backyard, regardless of how much money he was making from it. He was a dragon of science, a botanist, not a professor of comparative religions like his friend N'drn.

And yet, messengers from the Gods had done…*something*. No dragons had been there to witness it, at least none R'wn was willing to accept as credible, but there was no denying the change. The evidence of the Gods was everywhere. Had been for three years.

Before that, there had been random stories. Lights in the sky. Strange visitors in the forest. But this, this he could touch. Fly around, even. He had done so on two separate occasions, just to validate the science as he had explored the space within.

None of the Gods were known for geometrically-perfect

hexagons. Certainly not ones more than two thousand body-lengths on a side.

Most of the deities R'wn knew from his literature classes were better known for drinking and debauchery. Mathematics and science? Almost none, save for a few, minor ForgeGods worshiped in some of the northern nests.

But as R'wn glanced down at his armor's keel wedges, a second layer of scales made of a material he couldn't even begin to identify, there was no denying that *something* had happened. He had found the materials over in that forest. Markers of some sort, he and M'nth had theorized, from the strange writing on them. Perhaps identifying the various trees and bushes. Plates of black material bigger than any dragon he knew, but they had been able to find a few broken ones and eventually repurpose them by dulling several saws cutting the pieces into useful shapes.

The material was still impossible.

Light enough that he could wear brigantine plates of it on his keel and back when he flew, with almost no loss of speed or maneuverability. And the dorsal blade plates came with a pretty hieroglyphic printed in gold. The rest was a matte black so deep it seemed to drink sunlight, yet remained more flexible than vines, lighter than gossamer webs, and tougher than the best bronze M'nth had been able to pour yet.

Pity they had never figured out how to armor up wings and still fly. Not for lack of creative bullshit, failed experiments, and nights drinking mead freshly-made in fallmelon pods, mind you.

With better armor than the various bits he had cobbled together with M'nth's help, R'wn would have been willing to fly high enough to see the whole of the strange, new forest. Prove that a perfect hexagon had taken root in the middle of the otherwise-flat Trthn Meadows.

But there were eagles up there. A little dragon would be fresh meat that far out in the open.

And the petite bronze sword he wore in a baldric was useless against raptors like that. Perfect for beetles, and cracking open nut cases, but not really a weapon of violence, except by intent.

So where had this strange forest come from? Nobody knew. Of course, none of the other dragons flew this far east from the capital sanctuary at Krdn. Too big a risk of raptors overhead, or furred predators stalking the forest on the floor or in the branches. And there were plentiful fruit patches and hundreds of different species of bugs much closer to home.

That was why they paid a botanist so much for exotics.

Which, these days, apparently involved stealing from the Gods. The New Gods. The ones who caused whole forests to magically appear overnight. (His old maps definitively showed nothing here five years ago. Fuckers.)

R'wn shuddered from his snout to the lavender tip of his tail, tucked inside the godsmetal Seedhammer M'nth had made for him. Fools and poets loudly proclaimed that science was wrong and demons were in the process of ripping apart the veils between worlds, as the famous bard L'dn had predicted nearly eight hundred years ago.

Good dragons believed in science, not old wyvern tales.

R'wn took a deep breath and scanned the skies overhead. He always hated this part the run, several minutes mad flight across the open meadow before he was safe again in those trees over there. Could he call them trees? Nobody recognized the species, even in the oldest journals he had bribed a librarian to show him.

Tomorrow's problem. Today, he had to avoid eagles and harriers to get to his secret botanical station. Out there in the open, a periwinkle dragon stood out against the browns and greens of the meadow. Birds of prey weren't immune to his fire breath, but they were smart punks and knew to pounce on him from behind. Unarmored, R'wn would be killed instantly. Even with the godarmor, still probably wounded.

Best not to risk it.

At least with the sun up, he might see them coming. Night brought those damned horned owls. R'wn shuddered again.

Clear skies above. Minimal cloud cover as a storm front had passed yesterday. Nothing to do but to chance it.

He was off, flapping as madly as he could. To protect his eyes, the inner lid was closed, while the outer one blinked only occasionally. Risk of dry eye over the loss of farsight.

The life of a dragon.

Maybe M'nth could pour him some high quality glass to use as a third eyelid? Hold it in place with rabbit-leather straps while he flew so he could keep both lids open? Maybe a skull-cap as well? It would be naturally brown. Better camouflage. R'wn added it to the list of mad adventuring gear that every dragon needed.

Grass. Humps. Rose bramble. Brook. Herd of rabbits lounging in the morning sun. More grass.

Movement overhead.

R'wn blinked hard with both eyelid to wet things well, then opened both lids at once, squinting into the cold windstream.

Yes, flier above him. While it was shaped like a dragon, it was still half again bigger than the biggest eagle R'wn had ever heard tell of. Its hide was a bright, jade green, the rarest dragon color as well.

But dragons didn't have straight lines, anywhere on their body, any more than nature did. And the creature was gliding on perfectly straight-edged wings, with a straight, symmetrical torso that didn't wiggle at all in flight.

For a moment, R'wn forgot to flap, as he realized what the creature was. And that it had apparently seen him and was starting a roll to come this way.

R'wn calculated the distance to the edge of the trees, and wondered if he could out-run a God.

CHAPTER TWO

FAIRCHILD

THE PROBLEM with learning to be responsible was that you had to adult. Fairchild hated that part. But she figured that if she did a little adulting every day, then she could goof off the rest of the time successfully. That way, it didn't pile up.

And if being "Fairchild the Adventurer" continued to pay enough bills, then she didn't ever have to go back to being Lady Danielle Cooper. Yuck.

So today, she was adulting.

This planetary expedition was even more miserly than the last one, even with the galaxy-famous Fairchild on board, so they hadn't brought a heavy lander that she could fly. Plus, Dr. Montjoy and the Michigan State xeno-biology staff didn't want their precious research reservations disturbed.

Thus, Fairchild was up in a wingsuit this morning, rather than the free glider she preferred. Or the *Qunsahr Industries Shuttle, Mark 4, Heavy* that was her joy. She could still glide on thermals up here, letting the electric fans rest while she flew from Waypoint D to Waypoint E in the most efficient way she could. So she could get back to base and stop adulting.

Biysk was an *Earth*-like world, like so many of them, all apparently terraformed by the vanished race known only as the Elders. Everywhere people explored, lots and lots of friendly planets already existed where humans could walk on the surface without lifesuits. And sometimes even eat the local fruit or critters without being terminally surprised.

Until two years ago, those beings, the Terraformers, had only been theoretical, since no definitive proof had been found of an intelligent, tool-using, star-faring species. Before Fairchild's religion-shattering, accidental discoveries on *Escudra VI*.

Along the way, some genius had decided that humans should colonize *Biysk*, and funded Dr. Montjoy to explore her theories. To top it off, the rich madman was English, or at least had a black, English sense of humor. Below her was the oldest of the grafting hexagons that had been dropped on the surface over the last three planetary years, after robot landers had cleared and leveled spaces for them in different climate zones.

Yup, he had to be English. That was a Hundred Acre Wood below her. By design. Silly lark had designed a landership around a biodome with a biodegradable floor, so that they could drop it as an object on the surface of *Biysk*. Nobody even used acres as a measuring system any more. Everything was hectares.

But everybody grew up with Pooh Bear. Even Lady Danielle Cooper.

Fairchild checked the readouts on the Heads Up Display (HUD) projected on the inside of her wingsuit's faceplate. Nice morning. Mid-twenties now, high twenties later. Glorious. Clear skies with some high cirrus, soft wind out of the southwest. Paradise.

She had seen a few of the weird, local raptors, up for an early breakfast. Giant, streamlined butterflies almost, with two sets of wings and talons like birds. Dangerous, but she was bigger than them, even without the wingsuit, so they had scattered like seagulls as she approached.

"Wake up, Fairchild," a woman's voice gently intruded, grounding her back into an unhealthy state of adulting. "We're approaching the next waypoint marker."

Eleanor. The AI governess Fairchild had known since she was four. The electronic snoop, scold, minder, and best friend for nearly thirty years. Part of the reason she was still alive, most of the reason she was no longer crazy.

That crazy, anyways. Uncrazy people were boring. Stodgy. White-Picket-Fence.

Yuck.

Nope, better to be a little crazy. Just not so dark and on the edge of life-taking depression anymore.

And adulting only in small amounts, thank-you-very-much.

"Thank you, Eleanor," Fairchild replied.

Okay, so she might have been daydreaming, soaring over the slow, green river before entering the vast grasslands below to find a single, clean, hexagon of trees, like a rogue tile in the kind of world-building, table-top games she had played with her brother Rudy's kids.

Fairchild triggered the various sensors to upload their data. Cheap ignoramuses would fund a new class of lander ship, then scrimp on funds for a simple constellation of communications satellites for all the electronics. So somebody had to fly over and retrieve everything twice a week because the radios were all low-power. Stingy vultures.

Fairchild banked so she could get a better view of everything before proceeding on to Waypoint F. Two more hours of adulting and she was done for three days. And there was a cute botanical chick among the grad students.

Movement caught Fairchild's eye. Low to the ground but still flying. Moving like a javelin, too. Headed straight to the Hundred Acre Wood, which made no sense. That place was all *Earth* flora and fauna, a mass of fruit trees and bushes, plus all sorts of worms and bees and birds necessary to pollinate things and poop seeds over a bigger area, to see what could survive.

Nothing shaped like that in the manifest, or that particular color of neon purple. Teeny, too. Not even the size of a Norther Flicker.

"Huh," she muttered under her breath.

"What is it, Fairchild?" Eleanor asked.

"Critter," Fairchild answered. "Small, fast, and purple."

"So?"

"So I'm bored, and ahead of schedule," Fairchild observed. More adulting.

"Well, be careful, dear," Eleanor said tartly. "Or you might accidentally commit science again. Maybe become even more famous."

Fairchild kept her sarcastic reply to herself. She had accidentally discovered proof of the Elders, after all the effort those folks had gone through to hide their tracks before disappearing. Boffins in Norway kept nominating her for stuff. Fuckers.

She locked her sensors on the wee beastie and powered up her fans. The nav system began to bitch about being off course, but it was like that. All work and no play made the stupid thing happy. She reached up with her right hand and set the system to silent mode. She could fly this patrol in her sleep, after this many trips.

Free glider would have been more fun here. Just fall from

the sky and let membranes between limbs and body parachute her.

Wingsuits were a misnomer. The thing she was in was really more of a backpack she strapped on. Wings telescoped out over her shoulders. Elevons like peacock vanes above her butt with lateral posts you stood on to hold her feet up. Three powerful induction fans. About as smart as a squirrel, all by itself, but it was as close as she could get to true flight without her free glider.

And it paid the bills.

Pitch over and dive, just to give that little purple bird a good heart palpitation. He was running for trees like she was a hawk, which she probably resembled to a critter that small.

Fairchild let the sensors track it and dialed up the magnification. The shape was all wrong for the birds she knew.

Oh, COOL!!!

It was a teeny, little, pixie dragon!!!!

Weird color scheme, though. Neon purple head, hips, and tail. Lighter-colored wings. But the torso was flat black. She snapped a couple of pictures and fed them to Eleanor, waiting patiently in her little AI pod, currently tucked into the pocket between Fairchild's breasts. The most likely place to not get lost during a night of drunk partying. As long as Fairchild could find her clothes afterwards.

Beast was moving something fierce, too. Might have been an interesting race, but he had a hell of a head start and Fairchild was just goofing off. She sheared to one side as the little wyrm made it into the trees and vanished into a monstrous blueberry bush.

"Oh, dear!" Eleanor exclaimed suddenly.

"What?" Fairchild cried, craning her head all directions for a major predator about to jump out.

She powered all three fans to redline and stood the

wingsuit on its ass as the best way to confuse most creatures while escaping back into the sky.

"Oh, nothing dangerous, Fairchild," the governess intoned after a moment, with a sarcasm that few people other than Fairchild could ever truly appreciate. "That dangerous, anyways. You're probably going to have to be famous again."

"Why?" Fairchild asked in the sidelong, petulant voice of an eight-year-old having to go shop for clothes.

The wingsuit had enough height, so she backed off the engines before smoke started coming out.

Eleanor projected a still of the little dragon onto her right side HUD, then zoomed in tight. A quick enhancement wash for pixelization revealed a symbol on the black part of the dragon's back, just dorsal and aft of the right wing.

Fairchild let loose a string of profanities in several different languages as she recognized the thing in the image. She doubted the beast was a true fan, this far away, but there was no mistaking the Michigan State Spartans logo he was wearing.

CHAPTER THREE

R'WN

R'WN WAS JUST happy he hadn't brained himself on a low branch, flying full tilt into the strange bush and only pulling everything in tight at the last moment. Maybe when he asked M'nth to make him third eyelids, he should see if they could find any of that black godsmaterial that was curved enough for a helmet.

Botanists didn't do adventuring. They stayed in quiet places, growing and breeding plants. Still, if he wanted to be rich, he had to do crazy shit occasionally.

New Gods didn't help his peace of mind. At least this one hadn't caught him before he reached cover. Hopefully safety. R'wn scrambled up the trunk of another of the strange bushes and cowered on a branch, struggling to control his breathing.

He was alive. The New Gods weren't all-powerful, whatever they were.

Or they were just playing with him.

R'wn watched the being leap into the sky, stall elegantly, and then land in a roar probably good enough to scare every rabbit and squirrel in a thousand body-lengths, no more than thirty dragons-lengths away.

Crap, he had accidentally led this one right to his botanical research station. It would find out too much.

Perhaps he had accidentally awakened a guardian on his last visit?

Still, he was a scientist, first and foremost. If this was a New God, he would study it, even if he didn't do animal husbandry. Or comparative religions.

The monster landed lightly, stood for a second, and then *TRANSFORMED* into an erect quadruped.

Quadruped?

Double guano, maybe it was a demon or something, a bright, green monster from his worst nightmares, with one of those golden hieroglyphs on its keel in gold.

There was no way this was an accidental meeting.

Every other creature R'wn had ever encountered or studied was a hexaped, except for the servants of the New Gods, the strange, aggressive, winged creatures that called this particular forest home. The rest were generally his size, and had learned to leave him alone, once he defended himself a few times with fire breath or bronze blade. But they were regular-sized creatures. Animals of biological intelligence. Territorial, but not suicidal. Even the tiniest one, the beast with the long, slender snout, the flier that hovered in place while yapping angrily at him, had learned manners. Eventually.

This was a giant. R'wn estimated it to be at least nine dragons tall, covered with a leathery hide that glistened. And no face at all, just a smooth sphere for a head. R'wn counted. Four fingers and an opposable thumb on the two hands, rather than five and thumb, like natives to this realm.

R'wn pulled his paws up underneath and prepared to leap to safety if the creature spotted him. He could outrun it inside the forest, where those wings it had would be too wide, as long as the giant couldn't call on unseen servants to jump out and trap him as he moved.

It came closer, scanning right and left. Patient. Careful. Hunting. R'wn had seen the same behavior in the furred night hunters that occasionally strayed too close to the Krdn Nest.

R'wn held his breath as the thing approached. It didn't appear to have spotted him as it reached the edge of the forest, heading towards the bush he had flown through in his mad rush.

R'wn said a silent prayer to gods he didn't worship, thanking them for making him hide in this bush, rather than that one. Being prey sucked.

He nearly fell off his branch when the New God reached up its right hand and touched the side of its head. The smooth glass surface retracted three ways to reveal a strange face hidden underneath. Scaleless and flat skin, smooth and perhaps the color of pine nuts.

HELMET!

Of course. Was he dealing with technology? Nobody had ever proven magic, but some of the things M'nth built in her lab could fool the gullible.

A voice emerged from the New God. Deep and rumbly, unlike the chirps and whistles of people. A moment later, a second voice replied. The New God's mouth didn't move that time, so communication/response? Did it have a demon trapped in a magic necklace, like the legendary heroine N'tk?

Stranger and stranger.

The giant approached the bush. Berries were just at the verge of perfect ripeness, darkest blue skin, bright dragon-purple flesh inside. Tarter than most gourmands demanded when fresh, but they dried down and mellowed, or turned into a lovely, wine-colored jam or mead.

The two voices rumbled back forth for several rounds, before the New God plucked several berries, held them up in front of its face for a second in a strange way, and then ate them. Sniffing?

The sound that emanated from the creature was a purr so like a dragon that R'wn nearly fell off his perch in surprise.

Of course. It comes from that world, so it would be able to eat the fruits.

R'wn pondered the logistics of trans-dimensional invasions. Establish a base to feed your army, then strike? He felt his blood run cold at the thought. Maybe he should gather all the dragons up and burn this forest to ashes? Thwart the demons while there was still time?

The New God emitted a querulous chirp as its face snapped around, looking deeper into the woods. It started to move, walking awkwardly on those two, elongated legs.

R'wn cursed silently.

The New God had found his botanical station.

CHAPTER FOUR

FAIRCHILD

FAIRCHILD POPPED OPEN the faceplate on the wingsuit and took a deep sniff of the area. It smelled lovely here. Roses were in bloom, somewhere nearby, plus several other things that reminded her of what a home should smell like. She heard the tik-tik of hummingbirds emerge from the depths and laughed.

Necessary for botanical purposes, just like bees, but hummingbirds made lousy astronauts. Feisty, palm-sized T-Rexes who wouldn't take an ounce of shit from anyone.

"Should we radio for scientific assistance, Fairchild?" Eleanor asked.

Fairchild checked her clock and sighed. Still ahead of schedule. She could do a little exploring before she called in the cavalry. And the newspaper reporters.

"Not yet," she replied. "I'm hoping that we're just imagining things."

She took a couple of steps and studied the blueberry bush the pixie dragon had flown into. Nothing but lots and lots of huge berries, almost the size of grapes. She grabbed a handful.

"Is it wise to eat them, dear?" Eleanor queried.

"*Earth* soil, *Earth* bugs, *Earth* plants," Fairchild replied. "And Doc Montjoy says that they should be safe. I'm just conducting science here."

"Let me scan them, please," Eleanor ordered nicely.

Fairchild held them up where her helmet cameras could get a good view. Eleanor was tapped into the suit's feed.

"They look passable," the woman sighed after a moment. "And I can always fly the wingsuit home if you die of accidental poisoning here."

"I love you, too, Eleanor," Fairchild drawled.

She popped them into her mouth and munched. Yum. Fresh fruit on an alien planet was unheard of. But also part of the reason Teisha Montjoy and the MSU folks had gotten funding. Establish safe plants and a biosphere ahead of time, so scientists could identify what things grew on any given planet, and what future colonists could plant to survive on.

Blueberries were definitely working out here.

"Wazzat?" Fairchild asked suddenly, spotting something deeper into the trees.

She trudged towards a clearing a few meters behind the line of blueberry bushes, careful not to step on anything or anyone. That little pixie dragon was in here somewhere.

Strawberry patch. That's what it was.

Nature's loveliest weed, throwing invasive runners in every direction and offering to bribe you with yummy fruit for easement rights. These were tiny, though, way smaller than the kind Fairchild bought at the grocery. Each berry was only the size of the tip of her pinky finger to the first knuckle.

"Are those strawberries, Eleanor?" she asked out loud.

"Checking," the AI governess replied. "I believe so. Alpine. Thought to be the mother species from which all others were bred. Those look ripe, but stay away from the brown ones."

Fairchild knelt, thankful for the armored kneepads on the wingsuit. The first Alpine she grabbed squished in her hand, leaving a mushy mess. She licked it off her fingers and picked the second one much more carefully.

"Sweet," she observed.

"Theoretically, the same amount of sugars as a larger, commercial berry, dear," the governess said. "Those were bred up for size, color, and transportability."

"Huh." Fairchild sampled several more for quality assurance purposes. All seemed acceptable.

Beyond this patch of strawberries, a cleared patch of dirt caught her eye. Roughly a meter long and half that wide. Butted right up against the patch, but perfectly square, with straight lines furrowed into the dirt along the long axis. The existing patch was perfectly square as well, once she leaned back and studied it.

She flashed back to *Escudra VI*. Straight lines did not occur in nature. Even things that grew straight were only close. These might have been drawn with a ruler.

Fairchild held three fingers on the dirt, one in each of the first few furrows, and leaned forward so the cameras had a good field of vision.

"Eleanor?" she asked anyway.

"This might be your lucky day, Fairchild," her governess replied sweetly.

Fairchild growled the sort of words that would have gotten her mouth washed out with soap, back home on *Panamuer Nuevo*. Even today.

"I don't wanna be lucky," she cried. "I just want to fly and be free. I want to be *Fairchild*."

"Then you should stop letting your curiosity get the better of you, young lady."

Fairchild harrumphed loudly. She looked around and saw a flat shelf off to one side. Well, ledge. Pixie dragon bar height, if he went in for that sort of thing. Claw prints in the dirt looked right for a lizard.

She froze. Pulled her fingers into claws and then flexed them out again. Listened to the rabid pitter-patter of her heart racing.

Workbench. That was the word that sprang evilly to mind. A whole bunch of blueberries laid out to dry, covered over with some sort of mesh netting hanging loosely from a frame. And a thing that looked like a thimble, filled with seeds when she picked it up and peeked inside.

Fairchild sat it back down carefully and remembered to breathe. *Biysk* was a living world. Filled with all sorts of creatures generally built on a six-limbed model. Like her little pixie dragon.

But nobody had ever suggested intelligence. Tool-use. Planning.

Michigan State Spartans. Dried fruit. What looked suspiciously like a strawberry farm.

And…

"Fairchild?" Eleanor asked in a concerned voice.

"They're never going to let me live this down!" she anguished quietly.

"What, dear?"

Fairchild reached a tentative hand out and picked up a *thing*.

Call it what it is. *Tool*.

Short branch a little thicker than a matchstick, and a little longer. Polished smooth and turned on a lathe, to get that symmetry. And sticking out from one end was a brown, metal blade the size of her pinky finger. Edged on one side and slightly hooked, like a scythe, maybe?

Fairchild held it up for the cameras.

Eleanor gasped, which was saying something for an AI without any lungs.

"That's bronze, isn't it?" Fairchild whispered. "What is this thing?"

"What do you remember about your history classes, Fairchild?" Eleanor asked.

"I barely remember what I had for breakfast," she chided the woman.

"Fair enough," the governess said. "That looks like a primitive plowshare blade."

She projected a couple of images into the HUD for comparison.

Fairchild felt her heart sink. This was going beyond lucky. She wondered if she was cursed.

"Do you understand what this implies?" Eleanor continued.

"Probably better than you do," Fairchild replied. "Way too much adulting, coming up. Would you say this is pixie-dragon-sized?"

Long pause. Probably parsing syntax. It only seemed like the woman could read Fairchild's mind.

"Quite possibly, Fairchild," Eleanor said. "Should I call Doctor Montjoy?"

"No," she said firmly. "I did this. I have to own it."

"You'll be even more famous, dear," Eleanor warned.

"Don't remind me."

Fairchild set the rake-plow back where it had been leaned against the workbench and considered options. If the critter was intelligent, it was probably watching her right now. She would be. And up in the trees, invisible in the gloom, worried about Queen Kong rampaging through his strawberry garden.

She studied the blueberries. The seeds in the bucket looked like they had come off the strawberries, maybe scraped carefully so they could be planted in long, straight furrows beside her.

She had an idea.

"What are you doing?" Eleanor asked as Fairchild plopped down on her butt.

Tucked into the side pocket on the wingsuit/backpack was a Qunsahr Industries Emergency Pack, improved muchly after the last time she had needed to get into it, crash-landed back on *Escudra VI*. She skipped past the Tomya Manufacturing, Ltd. Survival Tool—as much as she loved the combination signal laser, fire-starter, flare gun—and went for the food pouch.

She had replaced the eighteen-year-old survival bars with stuff she actually liked, including a bag of granola mix. Fairchild pulled it out, and dumped a palmful of nuts and dried fruit into her mouth to munch.

See? Safe to eat.

She poured another palmful and set it on the workbench, next to the cage-thingee with the dried berries. The bag went into a front pocket on the suit so she could get to it easily later, along with the strawberry shortcake bar.

Strawberries for her Strawberry Dragon.

Carefully, she stood, and moved to the far side of the little clearing, all of two meters away, so she could sit with her back to an oak tree. Just for a security blanket, she pulled the survival tool and held it in one hand, set to fire-starting mode. In case the little pixie was angry, or rabid.

"There's food," she called in what she hoped was a relaxed, friendly voice, squirrel-crazy-girl in her head notwithstanding.`

Would he come?

CHAPTER FIVE

R'WN

IT WAS A TRAP.

Of that, R'wn had no doubts. The New God had found the berry patch he had planted only a week ago. And the dried bluefruits.

And the cultivator M'nth had sand-forged for him.

We are seriously fucked, now. Dragons discovered in the pantry of the Gods. Literally.

The New God continued its conversation through all this, speaking with the demon.

R'wn was surprised when it replaced the cultivator carefully. Perhaps the Gods were not offended by technology? He nearly fell off his perch when the being pulled out a pouch, ate a handful of what R'wn guessed were nuts and dried fruit from the color and scent, and placed a second handful on his workbench.

It moved carefully away from the bench, but sat in the open, so it obviously wasn't trying to hide. The voice chirped something.

It was a trap.

And yet, **SCIENCE!!!**

He could imagine no greater risk: to his life, his kind, and his culture. If they were demons intent on invading, it was his clarion duty to rouse the nest and bring them here to destroy everything with the binary phosphate spray each of them had as a defense against pissy eagles.

But this New God seemed to have technology. And the hieroglyph on its keel was the same as his dorsal bladeplate.

And they had brought strawberries into the world. R'wn had made good cash from fresh and dried strawberries, even as he had carefully retained the secret of their horticulture. Next year, he had planned to smuggle several dragonloads of soil outside the forest, to see if the berries could survive in this world.

It was still this world, right? He hadn't passed through a veil into the first plane of the abyss, had he?

R'wn wavered. He truly was present at the birth of a new theology.

Fuckers.

He could easily flee. Escape. Make it home safe and share his tale with M'nth. There was fresh mead nearly ready to lap up.

The New God would not take him.

And yet, **SCIENCE!!!**

The creature was obviously intelligent, if alien. It held a strange tool in one hand. A made thing. R'wn had no idea what it was, and it wasn't a blade, but the being's body language screamed weapon-ready.

But it also offered food by eating some first.

It is not poison I present. See, I have tasted of it.

Crap.

He was a botanist, not a diplomat. Still, sometimes you had to grab life with all twelve fingers.

R'wn crawled slowly backwards on the branch, and then

climbed down to the ground. He could launch from here, but the flapping of his wings would give him away.

Instead, he got up on clawtips and skittered madly away into the open, trusting the appearance of the New God to have scared away all the raptors.

He launched himself into the air, flapped madly for height, and banked. He had long-since memorized the pathway, in case he ever had to escape a flying predator into the forest.

R'wn found his path. He drew M'nth's bronze sword and shifted it to his right hand. He would need the more-dexterous left hand for the crazy-ass stunt he had in mind. Flying with the blade shifted his balance, but not enough to warrant doing this empty-handed. Every dragon needed their security blanket.

He charged.

Over the blue fruit bush, swoop-stall over the strawberries to lose altitude but not speed. Bounce once off the dirt with rear feet to throw off a bird tracking. Roll onto the left side, presenting the tougher back armor to the New God as he made a high-speed pass over the trap, snagging something so purple as to appear black in one hand.

Flying sideways curved him orbitally around the alien, but was also the best path between boles of the alien trees with the bark thick enough to hide fully grown beetles.

Start a swoop-stall again as a feint while rolling flat, yaw slightly, and take off straight up as hard as he could grab sky. Into the branches, where the risk was braining himself on something, while bursting through leaves big enough to sleep under.

Losing speed, but by design. Stall, pivot, pounce. Come to rest on a limb. Look down.

The New God hadn't moved.

Seriously? All that and the marauder didn't even react?

Fucker.

R'wn sucked air into his lungs and tried to not shiver too hard with the craziness of what he had just done.

He studied the thing he had snatched off the bench. Dried fruit by feel. Something that would be even bigger than the blue fruit when fresh, but dehydrated into a wrinkled, umber blob. It smelled sweet.

R'wn was a trained botanist, so he licked it. Sticky and syrupy.

He used the bronze sword to carve off a small piece, sniffed the interior, and tasted the morsel.

Not as good as strawberries. Better than the blue fruit. Probably not all that poisonous.

Hopefully, he would not see giant, pink eels dancing in the sky in a few minutes.

So, a peace offering from the New God? First contact?

Seriously, he needed a professor of comparative religions here. Or an Ombudsdragon. Somebody official.

And there wasn't anybody.

R'wn considered his options. He had his sword, a belt with a few tools, and his armor. Most of his gear was down on that bench, or back at the nest. Still, it had a weapon. He had a weapon.

And they shared a hieroglyph.

He took a deep breath, plotted his flight plan, and stepped off the branch to meet his doom.

CHAPTER SIX

FAIRCHILD

YUP, that was the pixie dragon. Periwinkle in this light. Fairchild had held her breath when he came, all set to make chicken tenders out of the little shit if he rushed her, but he had flown by, snagged a raisin, and vanished.

Reviewing the imagery she had captured and slowing it down had proven even more exciting, if you could call it that.

Little hooligan was holding a bronze sword in the hand that didn't grab the raisin. And was wearing what looked like a tool belt, with a sheath for the sword cross-draw, the way she would wear a shoulder holster for a pistol.

And maneuvering pretty intelligently to avoid traps. On his side, once off the ground, grab the raisin, vanish.

"Thoughts?" Fairchild muttered out loud.

"I am so glad that, as an artificial intelligence, I cannot be called on to testify, nor can I author scientific papers on the first intelligent alien species humans have encountered," Eleanor replied with the faintest frost of smugness. "Nor can I be held criminally liable for violations of any non-interference ordinances you've just broken."

"I love you, too," Fairchild replied.

This was about as adulting as it got. While the cute, grad student, botanist chick would be happy to talk to her now, Fairchild didn't see herself ever escaping Teisha Montjoy, the Michigan State Board of Directors, and probably whatever law-enforcement agency had authority over off-planet crimes.

"Who does have criminal jurisdiction, anyway?" Fairchild continued after a beat.

"Possibly the State Police of Michigan, dear," Eleanor replied after a long beat to thrash her database. "Maybe UNPOL, the United Nations Police. It would depend on the exact language of the charter covering this planetary expedition, of which I am unsure. We're in a bit of a gray area here."

Understatement of the year, thank-you-very-much.

Fairchild shrugged and clutched at the survival tool, just in case. Fresh chicken tenders, in self-defense, was a galactic crime she was willing to contemplate right now. There had to be more of the pixie dragons around, if they were stealing tree signs and boundary markers to make armor.

A flash of light brought the survival tool up.

Movement.

Strawberry dragon.

Not quite hovering like a hummingbird, but damned impressive for a winged, hexapodal lizard maybe eighteen centimeters long.

Cute, too, especially way he was holding that pixie sword out, point forward, mirroring her survival tool. Damned thing looked like it would be good for about two olives in her next martini glass.

He came to rest, half-sheltered behind the bar, staring intently at her.

Fairchild considered the wingsuit she was wearing. Not really armored, per se, but tough enough for most things.

Probably not enough to stop a flying gila monster taking a nip at her, but maybe enough for the claws.

She found herself leaned way forward somehow, so she tried to relax, enough that the backpack touched the tree again.

Hopefully, only one pixie dragon.

It chirped at her. And a quick whistle.

"Well, the folks in Oslo will probably be calling soon," Eleanor offered.

"Would you shut up, please?" Fairchild tried to keep her voice calm.

Calm enough. Little pixie was locked on her, maybe as fascinated as she was.

Sorry appeared on the HUD in bright crimson letters.

Fairchild took a breath and lowered the point of the barrel from the periwinkle intruder. Non-threatening.

"Hiya," she said in a bright voice.

The little man cocked his head just about like a Chihuahua her brother Rudy had once owned. It warbled something. Didn't sound like a dragon bellow. More like "Who the hell are you?"

But he lowered the tip of his sword. Down and to one side, just like her chicken-tender-maker.

Oh, what the hell?

"I'm Fairchild," she said, pointing to herself with her other hand. "I'm new around here and wondered about your strawberry patch. And the dried blueberries, and all the other stuff. Wanna chat?"

You have gone insane, the HUD said.

Nope. Already done that. This was nothing at all like trying to swim all the way to Hell on *Escudra VI*.

Pixie twittered. And sang. And chirped some more.

If she could understand him, it sounded all lovely. Or not. Maybe "Hey, lady, get your ass off my farm."

Fairchild considered all the classes in diplomacy she had slept through. Eleanor had been awake, but seemed less than supportive at the moment. Better to not ask her.

Or was it?

The one thing she had in common with the runt was that they both appeared to be Michigan State fans, to the casual voyeur. If there were any here.

"So, let's try something easier," Fairchild said as calmly as she could, pulling her feet under her like a cat so she could lean forward, without looking like she was about to pounce.

Periwinkle boy tensed and opened his mouth a bit, like he was going to bite her or hit her with fire, but remained still, both side eyes screwed forward, like a whale, or a chameleon.

Fairchild extended her left hand and put her index finger in the dirt. They were over two meters apart, so hopefully he wasn't that fast.

"Eleanor," Fairchild said. "I need you to project the Spartan logo onto the HUD so that I can trace it in the dirt here."

Rather than reply, the governess did. Greek style helmet facing right, with a brush on top.

Fairchild slowly pulled her finger along the image hovering on the left side of her vision. It was crude, but a pretty good representation. Hopefully, not an insult, or a proposition in dragon.

Pixie boy watched rapt. His mouth might have fallen farther open, but that had the look of slack-jawed surprise.

Still, she had his attention.

She added a few other things. A bad triangle, a square, a circle-looking thing.

She muttered as she worked. He chirped back. It sounded friendly.

Fairchild nearly wet herself when the dragon sheathed his

sword and squirmed around the workbench on all fours. Well, the four for walking. His wings were kinda half-mast. Maybe excitement. Or a threat exhibition. Possibly flight instinct. Hope to God not a mating display.

He moved down to the far end of the dirt patch and poised for a moment before sketching. Triangle, square, circle. Sword, maybe?

Fairchild replied with a stick figure human.

Pixie drew a dragon figure, much better than she could have. Kid was an artist. She could see the snout, wings, and claws on a long, lean body.

For fun, she wrote Fairchild in the dirt in blocky, English letters, and pointed at herself with her left hand. The one not holding the survival tool, just in case.

"Fairchild," she said, touching her chest, right where Eleanor was remaining quiet.

Pixie stared at her for several awkward seconds. Like, about time to run like hell? Or pounce?

Finally, he moved. One hand into the dirt. Three weird symbols separate from everything else.

Touched himself on the chest, like she had.

He warbled. It had two syllables. Sounded like a name.

"Ir-win," maybe.

Never, *ever* going to escape adulting now. Ever.

Fuckers.

Fairchild tucked the survival tool back into its pouch and pulled out the granola bag. She grabbed a dried cranberry and placed it between them, leaning quickly back.

Pixie studied her hard. Intent. Way more intelligent than Rudy's Chihuahua ever was.

Finally, it turned, plucked a fresh Alpine strawberry off a plant close by, and skittered out to set it next to the cranberry.

He picked up the dried fruit with his left hand, nodded

thank you at her, and waddled back to his side of the dirt patch.

Fairchild picked up the berry carefully, and tossed it in her mouth.

Pixie dragon noshed on the cranberry a moment later.

"Thank you," she said.

He warbled something back.

Carefully, she reached up and keyed the radio on the side of her helmet.

"*Biysk* Flight Control, this is Fairchild," she called.

"You vanished off radar, Fairchild," a man's voice drawled humorously. "Crash again?"

It was a running joke with those folks. To them, she was famous for crashing on *Escudra VI*, not for discovering alien artifacts.

"Negative, Flight Control," she said amiably. "Better."

"Better?" he asked, maybe just a bit nervous now. She was Fairchild.

"Yeah," Fairchild smiled. "Could you rouse Dr. Montjoy and tell her I've just ruined her afternoon?"

Fairchild smiled at the little strawberry dragon, perched now with his waist on the workbench and pulling some dried blueberries from under the netting.

Yup. Way too much adulting in the near future. But at least she'd be famous for not-crashing, this time.

PART TWO

THERE BE DRAGONS

ANN-MARTA WATCHED Dr. Montjoy put down the handset to the comm and mutter to herself. The woman was normally a golden tone from her Korean-American ancestry, but right now she was almost the color of snow. Hell of a contrast with Ann-Marta's dark walnut skin.

Teisha Montjoy opened her mouth and closed it a few times, like a surprised fish, before words finally came out.

"You were with her two years ago on *Escudra VI*," Teisha finally managed. "How would you qualify Fairchild?"

Ann-Marta leaned back and studied the wall behind Dr. Montjoy's desk. The paneling looked like wood, but was much lighter, having been imported because nothing on *Biysk* was cleared to be consumed yet, food or building materials.

This was a much longer-term mission than *Escudra* had been, so they had permanent facilities, but still had ended up hiring AM's company, Northmen Services, to handle ground services operations. Ann-Marta might look East African, but all of her grandparents had emigrated to Sweden, and she was viking to the core.

"Fairchild," Ann-Marta said as a placeholder, drawing up all the memories of that craziness, when the woman's shuttle died mid-storm and she bailed out. The search. The rescue that ended up rescuing Chike first.

The first solid evidence of intelligent, alien life in the universe, however long they had been gone.

Ann-Marta didn't really know Teisha Montjoy all that well. The previous contract for services had lapsed and not been continued with the folks who had apparently pissed the boss off.

She decided to answer the woman in honest terms, instead of dancing around the truth nervously.

"Fairchild is cursed by the gods, Dr. Montjoy," AM said. "At the same time, she is beloved by enough of them to offset that. It is as though they see in her rowdy impetuousness their own sordid youth."

"You think she really found intelligent aliens?" Teisha asked.

"Technically, we're the aliens here," Ann-Marta pointed out. "This is their world."

"True."

Dr. Montjoy leaned back now and seemed to be studying some unseen horizon.

"This changes literally everything," she mused.

Ann-Marta had to agree, but she probably had a deeper understanding of the legal clauses in the charter and hiring contract than Teisha Montjoy did. Occupational hazard, working with academics who tended to let the university's lawyers negotiate such things.

"I am also concerned that Fairchild won't allow a shuttle or large aircraft in the vicinity of her find," Montjoy said.

"Can you fly a wingsuit, Doctor?" Ann-Marta asked.

Not always a given with academics. Especially not middle-aged ones who might have forgotten all the rowdiness of their youth. Chike Odille, for example, before he got over himself.

"I can," Montjoy replied.

"Then you and I can fly out and meet Fairchild and her friend," Ann-Marta said.

Someone from Northmen Services would have to do it. Might as well not let Gavin or Andrea have all the fun.

"Just us two?" she asked.

"You will be safe," Ann-Marta assured her. "My people will be ready to intervene if called, I can promise you that."

"But we've just potentially made First Contact with an intelligent, tool-using species," Montjoy muttered. "Now what?"

"As with Dr. Odille at *Escudra VI*, I suspect that you will become famous," Ann-Marta said. "And the Spartans will gain a whole new raft of fans."

CHAPTER EIGHT

FAIRCHILD

FAIRCHILD PLOPPED her butt back down in the dirt, once she was done talking to Montjoy. Ruining that woman's day, her week, and possibly making her career.

There were limits to adulting. Fairchild would go down in history for yet another famous first, but she was in no way qualified to handle things from here. She had taken classes in law and diplomacy, but slept through most of them, skimmed the books before tests, and aced them.

Before promptly forgetting everything a week later.

Life had been better that way. You didn't wake up with existential dread at where you might be going, unless you couldn't find your pants.

"Eleanor, can you access the grid from here?" she asked, watching the strawberry dragon watch her.

"I can, but the signal is a little weak," her electronic nanny replied.

"Can you look up some of the legalisms involved?" Fairchild said. "Who might have jurisdiction for law enforcement, who takes over in the impossible case that a planet is found to be inhabited, that sort of thing."

"Yes, give me a few minutes," Eleanor replied.

Fairchild muttered to herself and leaned over so she could draw in the dirt again with her fingertip. She did another stick figure, and then added two more. Teisha Montjoy and apparently Ann-Marta Thorgisdaughter were coming.

She remembered Ann-Marta—aka AM—from *Escudra*. Woman ran a tight ship, charged with keeping all the academics and undergrads safe on the surface of a hostile planet, as well as finding them when anybody got lost. Fairchild would have expected Fahmida or Juan-Marco, since it was going to involve wingsuits, but anybody could fly them, so she supposed that the boss might have pulled rank.

It wasn't every day you got to meet a strawberry dragon.

Her friend waddled close enough to see what she'd done in the dirt. Seemed to process it pretty well, too, with something like a nod and a head wiggle about like she'd done a time or two encountering folks without a common language.

Language.

"Eleanor, can you decipher his language?" Fairchild asked.

"I'm sorry but no," the woman replied. "While I contain a vast number of human languages, or at least the ability for rudimentary communications in them, your friend is not something I was programmed for."

Well, crap. They were back to pantomime, weren't they?

At least Fairchild was pretty good there. Helpful when you wanted some tall, dark stud—or babe—to hit on you and take you back to their place, in spite of the language gap.

Fairchild considered the body language dilemma. Strawberry dragon had more limbs than her, and was studying her like he wanted to know where the party was headed to next.

Party games? Sure, why not?

She drew a flat line for a horizon and then the sun overhead. Montjoy and Ann-Marta would be here in about an hour, so she drew a second sun lower in the sky with an arrow from the first one, and then tapped the image of three stick figures again.

Something got through. Periwinkle suddenly perked up.

Shit, we're communicating.

Adulting, even, although adults would be utterly lost right now, unless they had kids. Or spoilable nieces and nephews in Fairchild's case.

Kid wasn't dumb, that much was obvious. Had a Bronze Age level of technology somewhere, but clearly wasn't native to this Hundred Acre Wood that had been grafted onto his planet. Size and the fact that he was growing strawberries inside the forest here suggested that his kind were probably native to one of the forests nearby.

Fairchild pointed at him and whistled querulously, just to see what he thought.

CHAPTER NINE

R'WN

HE CONSIDERED the image that the New God had scratched in the dirt with its gloves. Three figures, which suggested two more were coming, in addition to this one and its demon necklace that spoke.

The image of the star overhead moving suggested that they would be coming, but not immediately.

Thank the gods. The old gods. The ones that looked after the nests and protected them from cats, birds, and other predators.

R'wn had maintained his worry that this alien woods was on another plane of existence, and that every time he entered it he was crossing between worlds. If it would take them that long to get here, they were not omnipowerful.

Nor omniscient, if they had been previously unaware of his kind.

Alien. Of that there was no doubt. As a scientist, he had never encountered a species with quadrupedal stature. Walking looked awkward, with only two feet, because the upper two were definitely tool-handling.

He wondered if they were constantly falling over and had to stride each time to catch themselves.

Giants. Not quite ten dragons tall, depending on the technological helmet it wore. Perhaps as many dragons wide across the upper limb span.

The face had no scales, so R'wn suspected that to be the creature's natural appearance, with the rest being an armor of some sort, where the hieroglyph on the left side of the keel matched the one on the impossible material he and M'nth had chopped and cut to make his armor.

But the New God seemed to be telling him that more New Gods were coming. Here. Now, or at least soon. He needed M'nth and probably N'drn. M'nth because she would be all over learning new ways to forge things. N'drn, because even a professor of comparative religions needed to be knocked off his perch from time to time.

And all this was a new theology. Fuckers would probably make him a demigod before it was all over, just to be a boil on his tail. They'd start including him in theological stories with N'tk if he wasn't careful. But the new god facing him had a magical necklace with a demon bound in it, so he'd probably lose that argument with the academic boffins. M'nth would want to know how to make one dragon-sized, he was certain.

Dare he take the strangers back to the nest? What would new gods do? And would they offend the Old Gods who had forgotten to warn everyone about aliens?

Shit.

Then there was the risk that the new gods would destroy the nest entirely, in spite of this one being friendly. It might yet all be a trap.

He would have to risk something. Could he communicate with this strange creature with too-few fingers or limbs?

It wanted to communicate via dirt.
He could do that.

CHAPTER TEN

FAIRCHILD

SHE WATCHED her little friend move to a clear spot and brush it flat. They were staying away from his strawberry patch, but she could see them running out of clearing to write in. Would his fingers have the right electrical resistance that she could bring him a tablet to write on? Even the smallest one would have keys about the size of his hands, but that might make things really interesting. He seemed to have verbal language, which was fine.

The ability to communicate complex ideas via ideograms suggested that he had writing, as well.

"Eleanor, how closely does Bronze Age technology and written language coincide?" she asked.

The fact that her governess was an AI without lungs meant that the little gasp the woman gave was for her benefit.

Fairchild scowled at the woman's image in her HUD.

"I'm not stupid," she reminded Eleanor, again. "Lazy, yes. Immature, frequently. Unruly with the best of them. But not stupid."

"I have known you for more than twenty-five years,

Fairchild," she retorted. "You have surprised me more in the last two years than in all the rest before that put together."

"This morning, I was intent on adulting in a small-enough dose that I'd get to goof off for a few days," Fairchild reminded her. "Someone likes it when I adult. Except that then the world turned upside down."

Long pause. At least Eleanor wasn't going to argue with her on this one.

"The two topics seem to run reasonably close, Fairchild, with primitive written language, frequently ideogrammic in nature, coming first, but not by much."

Fairchild nodded.

She'd be willing to bet he had something like a proper written language, but that could wait at least a day.

Dr. Montjoy was a xenobiologist who specialized in botany. Nothing was going to prepare the woman for draconic Shakespeare, when it happened.

Periwinkle was a damned good artist. She recognized the image of the strawberry dragon he drew as him, down to the way his nose horns curved backwards. The other two dragons looked different enough to be individuals, and not even close relatives.

Was he suggesting that he go get some friends to even out the equation?

Shit. Now we're doing advanced diplomacy.

What the hell had she done in a previous life to earn this kind of karma, anyway?

He paused now and looked up at her. Cocked his head a little as if asking a question. Chirped in a way that she was beginning to understand mean *query.*

Why couldn't Dr. Montjoy get here faster, damn it?

She studied everything, suddenly back at that one bar with the cute redhead she didn't share any languages with, except when she'd leaned over and kissed the woman full on the lips. That had gotten through.

Fairchild studied the various drawings. Wiped out hers and then started over, with three stick humans and three really ugly stick dragons way out of scale to the point they looked like carnivorous butterfly monsters from a kaiju movie. She put the first sun in, and then a second one way lower, hopefully suggesting to her little buddy that they'd meet her friends for dinner and then his gang for drinks and a pub crawl.

Or words to that effect. Go with what you know.

Fortunately, he was muttering under his breath as much as she was, even if his sounded cuter.

"Fairchild, this is Ann-Marta," a voice suddenly broke her reverie. "We are zeroing down on your coordinates. You're inside the forest zone?"

Strawberry dragon had been studying her suggestion for a hot date, or something like that, but he froze when a new voice emerged from her speakers. So, good enough to identify individuals aurally?

But she already knew he was smart.

"Affirmative, Ann-Marta," she replied. "I'm going to stand up and walk out into the open. You two land nearby and we'll see what the strawberry dragon does at that point."

"Is he dangerous?" Dr. Montjoy was suddenly there.

"He's eighteen centimeters long, and half of that looks like tail, Doc," Fairchild replied. "He had a sword about as dangerous as the one I spear olives with for a martini. We've been discussing plans for dinner."

"You're WHAT?!?"

"Joke, Dr. Montjoy," Fairchild said. "Pantomime and sketching in the dirt. Trying to communicate complex ideas without even body language in common, ya know?"

She could hear the wingsuits now. That high, buzzing

sound when all three engines were running flat out trying to get you somewhere in a hurry.

Like, say, First Contact with an intelligent, tool-using, alien species.

The dragon had slithered back behind his bar, like he was expecting a brawl and needed cover.

Fairchild pointed to the sound, and then tapped the image of the three stick humans.

"They are here," she said quietly. Calmly.

Like trying to deal with a friend freaking out on some narcotics flashback that had the walls glowing pink and writhing.

Not that she'd ever undertaken illegal pharmacological extracts for such an experience. Honest.

She rose slowly and waved at him. Not a *come hither.* More of a *you hang here while I go get them* kind of thing.

He at least chirped. She counted that as a win.

Eleanor had been remarkably silent through all of this, but Fairchild had also noticed that when she did talk, Periwinkle tended to flinch. Maybe she had as well.

Bad juju?

She walked around the amazing blueberry bush and out into the open. Two Spartan green wingsuits cruising low and starting their stall/landing as she felt the afternoon sun on her face. Northern hemisphere. Southern edge of her Hunnert Acre Wood.

Her and a strawberry dragon.

Ann-Marta landed first. Way more graceful, like she did this routinely or something. Teisha Montjoy didn't hurt herself or anyone else getting to the ground. Call it a win.

Faceplates retracted. Korean boffin. East African Swedish Viking babe.

Fairchild just grinned.

"Had to top *Escudra VI*, huh?" Ann-Marta asked with a matching grin.

Fairchild shrugged.

"Always on to bigger and better, ya know?" she asked.

Montjoy wasn't quite stomping, but wasn't happy.

"Doc, he's a little skittish," Fairchild said. "We outweigh him by a whole bunch, and he's this long."

She held up both hands.

"Does he bite?" she asked breathlessly.

"Not so far, but this is only our first date," Fairchild replied automatically.

Ann-Marta bounced with suppressed giggles. Montjoy turned beet red. Eyes huge.

"Sorry, bad joke," Fairchild amended.

She'd already explained it all once, but that was like three minutes ago, and Fairchild knew how boffins could get.

"So he has this logo on his armor," she said, touching the Spartan on her left breast. "That was the clue that he was more than just a flier. Then I found a farm where he is growing strawberries. We traded dried fruit and chatted for a bit. I told him you were coming. He asked if he could go get some friends to even things out. I suggested later, but that was right when you got here. I'm hoping he hasn't spooked."

"Are there any dangerous creatures around here?" Montjoy asked, turning back and forth between the two of them.

"Besides us?" Ann-Marta asked, causing the boffin to blink hard. "These forests contain birds and various insects for pollination and dispersal. Given that he's into human horticulture, I'm guessing that the amino acids and such are at least compatible. Surveys have indicated any number of small predators, equivalent to eagles or housecats, but as I understand it you selected many of these areas for the lack of large predators, Doctor."

Fairchild was impressed. More impressed. Ann-Marta always knew her shit, but this was new shit. Apparently, the woman hadn't slept through the right briefings. Fairchild always figured she could get summaries from Eleanor later.

Up until today, all Fairchild had been doing was flying survey patterns for the teams. They could have done it with autonomous drones, but these were apparently things they wanted humans doing, so that subtle and important details didn't get missed.

Like the galaxy's smallest basketball fan.

"Okay," Montjoy said with a heavy breath. "I am not a zoologist. I do botany, with critters as tools to help my plants."

"May I make a suggestion, Doc?" Fairchild asked.

The woman looked at her hard, probably remembering things in personnel files that really represented a much younger Fairchild, but she nodded.

"You and I approach him slowly," Fairchild said. "Share some nuts and fruit. Draw pictures in the dirt. Ann-Marta stays kind of out here where she can watch for big predators, but I'm guessing he didn't have troubles in there if he could farm."

"Are you sure you weren't replaced by an alien at some point?" Ann-Marta asked now.

"It might explain a few things," Fairchild laughed. "But no, Chike and a few others might have suggested that I should grow up at some point. Working on it."

"This is not earning you adulting credits that will let you slack off tomorrow, Fairchild," Montjoy said. "Your name goes on the report and the study as lead investigator."

But she had a smile on her face. So maybe she'd been paying more attention to the team and the project than Fairchild had thought. Enough to know her wingsuit pilot's tendencies, anyway.

"Lovely," Fairchild replied sarcastically.

Just what she needed. One of these days, somebody was going to dig deep enough to find the woman behind the name Fairchild. She'd warned her father so that he could sic his attorneys on folks.

Alphonse Cooper was not a man to be trifled with. Hell, his legal staff had probably enjoyed themselves, threatening any journalists starting to dig into the life of his youngest daughter. They were like that.

But if Lady Danielle Cooper kept doing famous-making shit like this, one of these days it wouldn't be enough to just tell everyone her name was Fairchild.

She'd gone ahead and legally changed her name before coming to *Biysk*. Good thing, too. The number of men and women proposing to her was going to skyrocket again. Not that she minded the cute ones.

She sighed, though. Nothing good was going to come of this. Her picture on the cover of every newspaper and magazine in existence just meant that she'd probably never have to buy her own drinks again. Small victories.

"Let's go," she said, turning back to her buddy.

And her destiny.

CHAPTER ELEVEN

R'WN

R'WN WATCHED from the cover of the blueberry bush. Two more had arrived, with the same apparently holy icon hieroglyph on the keel. Retractable faceshields. Wings that collapsed and folded into housings.

SCIENCE!!!

TECHNOLOGY, even!!!

M'nth would be beside herself with joy, no matter how many theories of metallurgy were about to be tossed into the fire.

First New God spoke with two others but the demon remained silent. God Two had skin more golden and darker than One. Three was the color of bark.

But weren't the dragons an example of all the variety of color available? R'wn counted this as a win. If the two newcomers had been identical to the first, then he would have known they were all demons after all and that this was a trap.

A bigger trap.

If there was such a thing.

The New Gods were about to displace ALL the old gods in one go.

And N'drn was going to blame him when the man was suddenly out of work. Or forming a new religious infrastructure, which was probably worse.

They spoke. R'wn recognized the voices as having come from the helmet of One. Some sort of method of communication that crossed all distances? Light had to be straight, but some had proposed that light, heat, and the sun's rays that caused trees to grow were all part of a single field of scientific endeavor.

What if one of the kinds of ray didn't have to be straight? And could go through things? Heat got largely blocked, but still made it through. Maybe there was a way to send sound?

All those classes in applied theology he'd skipped as a kid probably wouldn't have helped with this situation, either.

One and Two approached slowly. Three remained behind, like a guard intending to keep those pissy and inquisitive eagles from bothering things.

Did the New Gods breathe fire?

Closed helmets suggested not. Plus, they didn't really fly, not having dedicated wings. The first one had a made thing that it held like his sword, for all the round compactness.

It still screamed weapon. Danger. Stay back.

R'wn hopped off the branch and glided quickly back to his botanical station, taking up a spot on the other side of his workbench where he could bolt backwards into another bush with a lot of thorns to escape anything coming after him.

No snakes had colonized this hexagon that he was aware of. Just those strange birds with too few limbs and a variety of new insects that did follow the hexapodal model he was familiar with.

The newcomers made a lot of noise when they walked.

But then, their feet were almost bigger than he was, and they weighed like mountains, so moving quietly might be impossible for them.

One emerged and stopped at the edge of the clearing, shifting to its left and kneeling.

That was a weird way to sit, folding your legs in half and then putting all your weight on them. Predators did that, because they didn't have anything to fear.

Apparently, so did new gods.

Two wasn't as limber. Heavier-looking, or at least wider and rounder. It sat on the middle hinge and crossed those impossible legs at ankles.

You people are weird.

One leaned out and put a couple of nuts and dried fruits in the space between them, after munching a few from the same bag.

R'wn understood that they had to start over from scratch. Perhaps the newer New God didn't believe the first one?

Shit, would he, if N'drn told a similar story?

At least they had a whole raft of new fruits to work with. R'wn wasn't sure if all of them grew here, but the ones he had traded for so far had all been pretty good.

He grabbed a dried bluefruit and one of the dried strawberries and waddled out to the spot next to the other fruit, dropping his and looking up at the newer god.

"Welcome to my botanical station," he chirped happily at them, pausing to sniff the fruit on trade.

One was a sour berry from the smell. The other was a sweet chip that looked like a wood shaving enameled carefully. Useful as a shield, if he could find a way to mount some straps on it, but the New God thought it was food, so he carried it back to the bench and put it on top.

Two had gasped. Huge intake of breath that sounded a lot like someone about to breath fire and nearly sent him straight up into the leaves overhead, but it looked like an autonomous reaction to stress or fear.

He wasn't getting angry vibes off of them.

The New Gods chattered quietly at each other, so he grabbed a knife and went to work on the wood shaving, one eye tilted back towards them and the other down as he worked.

Gotta be careful not to draw blood. This bronze is sharp enough to penetrate scales.

The wood shaving was brittle. So not wood. Dried, but something that had a high fiber content and the ability to lose all fluid for storage. That might be useful for winter, given the apparently high sugar content he could smell.

R'wn remembered that he was a botanist, so he licked it once.

Yes, lots of sugar locked up in there. The New God had been eating them directly, so either the creature had enough saliva to break it down, or would regularly drink water. He had seen something put in the mouth that looked like a water gourd.

But he had company.

R'wn put the knife down after he got a shaving loose and put it in his mouth. They must have teeth like a herbivore in there, in spite of the sharp ones he could see. He gnashed on it a bit and managed to soften it up as he skittered around his bench to the spot where he had been exchanging ideograms with One before.

Just for the hell of it, he paused and wiped the entire field clean again. Nice, flat dirt. A few shades too brown for his tastes, but it was from an alien world, so it must be what they liked.

He grumbled at the thought of sharing his world with more gods, but he suspected that they had already defeated the entire draconic pantheon in order to be here, so he was just going to have to deal with it.

Hopefully, they weren't expecting a dragon of science like him to turn into some sort of bizarre messianic figure. The last thing he needed was to start transcribing a new religion onto some wood tablets and trying to convince M'nth and N'drn that he wasn't stoned out of his gourd.

You know what? Let's put you gods on a level playing field.

R'wn turned and etched the ideogram that he thought self-identified One. It was a weird scratching with low symbolic value, as near as he could tell, so perhaps they were advanced enough to use letters to form words, instead of embedding so much of their cultural references in the symbology.

Next to it—not below, not above, mind you, but *next* to it—he wrote his own name.

Then, to be a first class scientist and not a prophet, he tapped One's name and pointed at it, then his name and pointed at himself.

One laughed. Or something like that. It sounded joyful.

Two might be having a medical event from the pained gurgling emerging from its non-existent snout.

R'wn retreated to the side of his workbench and let those fuckers come to grips with their own theological complexities.

I am a dragon of science, mind you. Demons from the web have no grounding in scientific reality. Everything you do can be explained by rationalism.

I just have to figure out how.

He really needed M'nth's rednecking right now. And N'drn's experience with comparative religions.

And a drink. The mead was just about perfect right now.

Tapping a foot right now sounded rude, so he just paused, poised to flee like mad if he'd gone too far with Two, in spite of the way One was reacting.

One leaned forward and he nearly wet himself.

It reached out a claw and delicately erased part of the ideogram he had drawn, correcting it.

Ah, got a letter backwards. Not bad for a foreign alphabet from memory.

He nodded.

"Thank you," he chirped at One.

It warbled something deep back, then turned to Two.

Two seemed to recovering.

Maybe Two was having theological issues as well?

Shit, he'd never considered that.

Had they dropped this stupid hexagon of foreign soil and trees on his world and never once considered that people might already be living here?

You'd think New Gods would be smarter than that, but then he stopped and considered some of L'dn's stories of N'tk and the demons.

But if the gods were just people scaled up with power and hubris, regardless of the weird-ass biomechanics involved, then maybe they'd looked for other upright quadrupeds and dismissed the forest dragons? Especially at that size.

If they'd been talking to the eagles, R'wn could see that outcome. Those feathered punks lied about everything.

Still, he maybe needed reinforcements here. And leading them straight to the nest just sounded like the dumbest idea he'd had this week. Who knew what the gods might do at that point?

Of course, were they really gods? That was even more frightening, if he were to consider them some sort of sky barbarians who had just decided to move into the neighborhood.

How many of them were there? Could they destroy the whole nest? Or would that many pissy dragons breathing fire be too much for even New Gods to deal with?

Science suggested that they might fall for it once, but that they likely had tools far in advance of anything R'wn could lay hands on. M'nth's bronze sword was great for cutting leaves and cracking nuts, but the New Gods had longer fingers. Blunt, but longer.

Any one of them could squish a little dragon in one mighty hand if they ever caught him.

Shit.

But One wanted to talk. Had talked. Slow, complicated, not that great an artist, but earnest.

Could he break through the language barrier?

Fuck it. Let's find out.

R'wn moved to the other end of his black field and considered. One was a visual creature. Stereoscopic vision with two eyes directly forward, so some sort of alpha, pounce predator. His eyes were on either side of his skull, because eagles.

But it thought symbolically.

He drew a hexagon. Added a little x for the botanical station, and three stick God figures like One did them. And a stick dragon.

He paused and looked. One seemed intent and helpful from the body language. Two seemed to be breathing too fast and muttering under its breath.

Hey, pal. New Gods goes both ways here. Have theological controversies on your own time.

But he didn't warble that out loud. His mother HAD raised him better than that.

One nodded. He hoped it was a nod. Head up and

down. Mouth was way more mobile than his, but the eyes were pretty good at communicating. Black with blue rings around a circular iris, which was just weird.

Alien. Just admit it. They were not of this world.

How many worlds were there?

How many angry prophets and established religions were going to be banging on the mouth of his cave shortly, demanding recompense for the shit he was about to cause?

That alone almost made it worth it. Plus, they could explain to M'nth how to make this impossible, black material she had chopped and shaped into armor for him. Including the hieroglyph that seemed to communicate to all the New Gods on a different level.

Oh, the trouble he was about to unleash.

Carefully, R'wn wiped a claw across the dragon figure, leaving the three god figures untouched. He drew a better representation of a forest dragon outside the hexagon, facing away.

He did not, however, have it flying anywhere close to the straight path back to his home forest, although that wouldn't be that hard to figure out. But home was a big, dark place. Hard to find hiding dragons in there. Ask those stupid eagles or the bobcats that.

He drew wind into his lungs and studied One. Got a nod, like maybe that God was following all this. Two was a little dense, maybe? Or just theologically convulsed.

R'wn had been there. He could commiserate.

Later.

He returned to the hexagon he'd sketched and this time drew three dragon figures. Him, M'nth, and N'drn, although the professor might have to be dragged kicking and screaming, if R'wn told him any portion of the truth.

Probably needed to sneak up and pounce on him.

Maybe just tell him and M'nth that he had a fantastic surprise for them, at his botanical station, that was too big to carry home?

Technically even true.

The best kind of truth.

He sat up and crossed his arms at One, both eyes focused forward on the new god to see what it thought.

More warbling. One had a higher voice, but whether that was normal or excitement was impossible to tell. Two was deeper, but that might be existential dread.

R'wn stood his ground when One leaned forward slowly. Rapid movement and he'd hop sideways and see how fireproof they were, but One was minding the same manners.

A claw came out and added an image of the sun to the picture, roughly where it was now after a quick glance up. Pretty accurate location, actually. Did they have some sort of mechanism that counted time perfectly?

Oh, what he could sell *those* for, back at the nest.

Shit, it wants to know how long. That was how we did it earlier to discuss this.

He considered.

Race home like all the eagles in the world were on his ass. Find M'nth at her forge experimenting first. Grab her and kidnap N'drn. Fly back at a sane rate, because if he moved too quickly, they might decide he was up to no good.

Worse no good, anyway.

Call it mid-afternoon, because he'd need to grab some dried beetle meat and a flask of water or the thing of mead. Trouble, because the eagles were usually out in the late afternoon looking for their own dinner, so he needed to stay in the alien hexagon tonight. Blankets? Or just pluck some leaves. The alien ones with three blades tended to wrap nicely.

Here goes nothing.

R'wn waddled over and added a mid/late-afternoon sun to the image and looked up at the hyperventilating New Gods.

CHAPTER TWELVE

ANN-MARTA

ANN-MARTA GOT Fairchild's message that her strawberry
dragon was about to fly off and not to hassle or chase him.
She watched him go, emerging about three meters up and
then flapping like mad, an arrow with wings going like hell
towards a native forest that covered the lower part of this
valley where a couple of creeks eventually ran together into a
small river.

She wondered if strawberry dragons would nest close to
the water. Humans did, because of the value as a trade and
transport corridor to low-tech civilizations.

But humans didn't fly.

"He's gone," she announced over the radio. "Safe to join
you?"

"It is," Teisha replied.

Her voice was shaky. Must have been good.

Ann-Marta made her way through the first run of brush,
along a line still mathematically straight showing where *Earth*
soil and native stuff had not yet mingled, although some of
the plants seemed to be sending runners.

But wasn't that the whole point of this experiment?

She paused and grabbed some blueberries off the bush. These were almost grape size, so they liked it here.

Fairchild and Teisha were around a clearing maybe two meters by one.

"What did I miss?" she asked.

Fairchild practically glowed. Ann-Marta had seen that same look on her face a few mornings after a particularly good tumble the night before. Or maybe a good wakeup kiss.

"An intelligent, tool-using species of pixie dragon," Fairchild said.

"Dr. Montjoy, are you okay?" Ann-Marta asked.

Teisha was the color of golden snow right now.

"Huh?" she asked blankly. "Oh, right. Yeah. Do you have any idea what this means?"

"Actually, I do," Ann-Marta said, shooting a grin and a glance at Fairchild, who suddenly felt reality crash down on her shoulders.

Escudra VI, all over again. But even bigger. Too bad Chike wasn't here to deflect a lot of attention off the younger woman, like he had before.

Ann-Marta turned to the two women.

"How soon should we send the ship home with news?" she asked simply.

As Ground Services Coordinator, Ann-Marta would be responsible for making sure all the visiting dignitaries, reporters, and whoever else had accommodations. Plus, that none of them wandered off into the bush without adult supervision, looking for strawberry dragons.

There weren't many megapredators on this planet, but science had only spent a few years studying *Biysk*, so Ann-Marta was certain that some fauna had hidden.

That was why she was armed. Nothing flying around here was bigger than a large vulture, so she wasn't concerned about that. None of Fairchild's Golden Eagles from *Escudra VI*, although the woman had argued against that name.

The reporters had run with one of Chike's offhand comments and that was the end of it.

Teisha had frozen. Fairchild looked like an eight-year-old with a hand still in the cookie jar.

"If I may?" Eleanor the electronic governess spoke up now.

Ann-Marta nodded. She remembered the woman.

"I have been reviewing the relevant legal documentation," the woman continued. "While I am not a lawyer, I have some programming for legal situations and interpretations thereof."

Ann-Marta nearly laughed out loud. She would need it, if just to keep the Fairchild Ann-Marta remembered from *Escudra VI* out of trouble.

"Go ahead."

"The botanical survey contracts for *Biysk* do not contain formal language governing First Contact, as no human-like aliens were detected by initial scouts," she said.

"That leaves the UN," Ann-Marta said. "Which treaties govern?"

"I think just the Treaty of Cardiff," Eleanor offered hesitantly.

It was hard to remember that the woman was an AI. Whoever had programmed her had done an amazing job making her sound human, but she was also nearly thirty years old at this point, so had a lot of uptime, and had likely spent a lot of it in situations most prim and proper children would not believe.

Ann-Marta knew some of Fairchild's stories.

"Just Cardiff?" Ann-Marta asked.

"I am not a lawyer, Madam Thorgisdaughter," Eleanor

said in a more formal tone. "I can offer research advice, but cannot testify."

Fairchild had risen and was pulling Teisha to her feet, but the doc looked shaky.

"Good enough," Ann-Marta noted. "What are our immediate restrictions and concerns?"

Cardiff had been signed very early in the interstellar age, when humanity was just starting to explore other stars. No radio signals had indicated other life forms out there, but the Elder Race had supposedly been gone for so long that all their radio signals would have gone beyond the edges of the galaxy by now.

That left humans. And strawberry dragons.

"As they appear to be a Class III species, the planet is to be isolated until UN representatives can arrive," the woman replied. "Contact is to be kept to a minimum, but not cut entirely off. Interpretations of these paragraphs are squishy at best, if this outsider may observe. It appears that everything is removed from local control. I'm sorry, Dr. Montjoy."

Ann-Marta would not have believed Eleanor wasn't just a woman on the radio from the way she spoke, but again, someone with a lot of money had made sure that Fairchild had such an advisor. Ann-Marta had never bothered peeling away the layers behind Fairchild's past, as all the woman had ever wanted was to fly and occasionally seduce various members of ground crews or students. But nothing outrageous.

Consenting adults, as it were.

"Can we continue the research projects?" Teisha asked, giving voice to that woman's greatest fear.

The Hexagon Project was intended to make her career. Bad luck might end it.

Would the UN demand that all the stations be ripped from the surface of *Biysk* so that the planet could be returned to as close to a normal state as possible? Ann-Marta seemed to remember that Cardiff allowed it, subject to a variety of legal paths.

Eleanor paused.

"I appreciate that you cannot give legal advice," Teisha said, gaining strength. "Can you offer interpretations?"

"If I read this correctly, Dr. Montjoy, until such time as the UN representative arrives and says otherwise, the project leader—*you*—makes those determinations," Eleanor replied.

"And I will need to dispatch *Beagle* as soon as possible," Teisha said, mostly to herself before turning to Ann-Marta. "Can I turn certain things over to you?"

"Such as?"

"We'll need to get everything we can off CTSS *Beagle* before it goes," Teisha explained. "Supplies, spare equipment, all the shuttles except one for them, et cetera. If they are gone, we need to be self-sufficient here for however long."

Ann-Marta considered. She was relatively new to the contract, the previous holders having done a piss poor job of it to get themselves fired. Fairchild was technically one of her employees, although the woman had been seconded to the research teams so they didn't have to fly boring survey passes.

"I will need perhaps as long as three days, Dr. Montjoy," Ann-Marta decided. "It depends on a quick inventory I need to run when we get back."

"Is that something Lacumaces can handle?" Teisha asked. "I'd really prefer to keep you here with me. If the dragon won't be back until mid-afternoon, we might be camping."

"Understood," Ann-Marta said.

As if you could drag her out of here with a team of horses.

But she had good people, all of them veterans of *Escudra VI* and several other field projects. And many of them had been military special forces of various flavors, against the day humanity ever ran into another interstellar species.

"If our friend is going to be gone a while, might I suggest we do a quick hike to the lake at the middle of the hexagon?" Ann-Marta said. "We can refill water, survey things, and be back before he is. And I can talk to my people and start the ball rolling."

"Thank you," Teisha said simply.

Ann-Marta could see the color returning to the woman's face, but she was a botanist, not a diplomat.

"This way," Fairchild piped up, as if she knew where she was going.

But then, she'd flown this circuit every few days for several months, looking for things out of the ordinary.

If some of the gods hated the woman, at least others loved her.

CHAPTER THIRTEEN

R'WN

R'WN LANDED on a limb to catch his breath. That might have been a record crossing time. He would need a time-keeping machine from the aliens so he could start tracking those, one of these days.

Nobody had followed him. At least from a low enough altitude that he could see, flying or resting. But who knew what New Gods might be capable of.

Were they really gods? Or really freaking huge barbarians? N'drn would argue the former, probably, but R'wn was pretty sure the professor was wrong this time. Big and dangerous, sure, but technological sophistication didn't make them gods.

He sucked down another breath and hopped off this branch to glide. There was a safe path. You had to stay above the cats on the ground and below the things lurking in the treetops, but the evergreens tended to be bare trunk for a considerable stretch of elevation, so he just had to not fly slow enough that something hanging from the back of a tree could pounce on him.

This wasn't the way to the nest, because he'd taken a wide detour vector. Slower, but if they did follow him to the edge of the trees, they'd be headed the wrong direction.

A hard run in the shadows got him close. Past the usual scouts watching for predators and the foragers out looking for new bug nests to harvest or sudden mushroom events.

So far, so good. He warbled a few greetings as he went by, but didn't stop to chat. Sunlight was burning.

The smell was the first thing he noticed as he got close. M'nth was sand-casting today. Charcoal, glass, and bronze smell all mixed up. Her shop was down by the pond, where she kept a full cistern of water handy to douse everything if the fire ever got out of control.

R'wn glided in and circled once to make sure she wasn't doing anything dangerous before he landed. Tool of some sort from the steam coming out of the sand. Her cauldron was empty right now and she'd poured something in the sand to shape and cool.

She looked up and smiled at him, smudges of soot and dirt covering her jade-green scales and black working apron.

"Heya," she called. "What did you bring me?"

Shit. He'd promised her some of the dried bluefruit and completely forgotten it.

At least he had a pretty good excuse this time.

R'wn stalled and landed with a hard flap before waddling over close.

"You wouldn't believe me," he said as he planted a kiss on her cheek.

Informal. Friendly, even. She was no more interested in settling down and starting a family than he was, occasional romps notwithstanding.

"Oh?" she asked, stepping back to study him. "What evil have you done now?"

Okay, so maybe she knew him pretty well, after all.

R'wn shrugged innocently.

She laughed full-throated.

"Are you capable of leaving all this?" he asked, gesturing to the empty cauldron, the small pit of coal, and the bronze cooling over in the sand.

"What did you have in mind?" she asked, kind of sidelong.

"There is something at the botanical station I want to show you," he said. "It's too big to carry back here, and I want it to be a surprise."

"This late in the day?" she asked, surprised.

"I thought we might overnight there," he said.

"Oh, you did, did you?"

R'wn felt his scales flex outward in embarrassment.

"Not like that," he said. "Well, maybe not just like that, if I thought you might be amenable. But this is kinda huge. I was planning on dragging N'drn along as well. He needs to see it."

"So you aren't asking me out on a date?" she asked, possibly disappointed. Possibly teasing.

You never knew with M'nth.

"Not just a date, maybe?" he amended himself. "Serious, M'nth. I made a discovery. I need you and N'drn as witnesses. And consultants."

"Consultants?"

"It's big," he said. "Plus, N'drn might never forgive me, and I figure you'd want to see the look on his face."

Not that a metallurgist and a professor of comparative theologies *ever* argued about things. Perish the thought.

"What are you up to?" she asked, turning serious.

"It is a surprise," he said simply. "Worth your time. Might even make your whole week, if I can be so bold."

"Uh huh," she retorted. "Overnight?"

He nodded, holding his breath.

"I might insist on snuggles," she demanded.

"Gosh, the horrors," he grinned at her.

She grinned back.

"You go roust grumpy and I'll start putting all this to rest," she decided. "Then you can show me your surprise."

He kissed her again, before she could dodge, except that she didn't seem to be evading him.

"Back in a flash," he said.

And he was off.

N'drn had a nice cave, part of the college berm where all the instructors and staff generally lived. The quad was bustling with students, sprawled out or sitting up and actually listening to various lectures, depending on their nature. R'wn looked around but didn't see N'drn, so he swooped over and landed on the man's porch.

Others had handy rocks or shells you could bang together to announce visitors, but M'nth had made him a wind-chime of bronze bars, skinny and flat and different sizes. R'wn ran his claw through it a few times.

"Who is it?" a gruff voice called from down the hole.

"Tax assessor, come for your shit," R'wn yelled.

"Got your fireproof armor on, bucko?" N'drn yelled back.

"We haven't really tested it, N'drn," R'wn yarped at him. "Might need to."

A shadow appeared finally.

"What? No mead? Philistine."

N'drn's scales were more of a maroon with some orange thrown in. He was longer and a little heavier than R'wn, but that was partially the role of a stuffy academic who didn't spend nearly as much time in the air, nor flying great distances to harvest alien fruit for the botanical market.

"Got something better," R'wn said casually.

N'drn's blue eyes got narrow and both circled forward to stare at him.

R'wn was struck at how close the color was to the first New God, except that the being's eyes were just white orbs with black centers and a blue ring in between, instead of all one color.

How did they see, anyway? Predator vision, so probably flexible lenses. Did the iris open annularly? He made a mental note to ask, when they had enough common language.

Then laughed at himself.

"What's so funny?" N'drn demanded. "Come in."

He withdrew and R'wn followed. Quartz crystal in the walls and ceiling let light in and kept predators out. N'drn took his favorite bench and more or less flopped across it. R'wn took the one closer to the front door.

"I need your help," R'wn explained. "I have already asked M'nth to join me for an overnight stay at the botanical station, because there is something I have discovered that was too big to bring back to the nest."

Figuratively, as well as literally, since he didn't want them walking or gliding here, nor even knowing where *here* was.

"And you think I can help?" N'drn said. "A theologian, a metallurgist, and a botanist walk into a bar? Sounds like a terrible joke, R'wn."

"The punchline will be worth it," R'wn grinned.

"Scamp," N'drn retorted. "And knowing you, I will not get another word out of you, will I?"

"Oh, '*I told you so*,' maybe," R'wn laughed.

"What terrible thing have you discovered with the aliens?" N'drn asked.

R'wn went cold.

"Aliens?"

"That hexagon, as you have reminded me, is unnatural," N'drn stated. "Nature abhors straight lines, and a perfect hexagon that just appears one day out of the blue cannot be of this world. Ergo, aliens, gods, demons, whateverisms. What manner of truth remains to be seen, but they must be like us to some extent, given the wine and dried fruit you have been making good money supplying."

Okay, so maybe the old man had been paying more attention than R'wn had thought. But there was a reason he was a professor, after all. Big brains, and all that.

"Oh," R'wn replied. "I'm afraid that it would be much easier to show than to describe. I've asked M'nth to join me on a camp out and was hoping I might inveigle you into going, as well."

The dragon's eyes got serious. Focused. Scales went streamlined and everything.

"Does she know yet?" he finally asked.

"Nope," R'wn grinned. "*Way* more fun this way."

"But not dangerous?"

"Not so far," R'wn replied. "I am taking my sword, and you breathe fire last time I checked. Plus we can all fly."

"Truth." He lapsed into silence. "What should I pack?"

"Some food," R'wn replied. "Perhaps a journal if you wished to jot down some observations. Weather ought to remain pleasant tonight, and there is a particular alien leaf that I have found to be warm to sleep under."

"Someone better be bringing the mead," he enunciated clearly.

"I will make sure one of us packs it," R'wn assured the professor.

"And that's it?" N'drn asked. "All you intend to tell me until I am face to face with whatever monumental discovery you think justifies taking me away from my studies and writings for a day or two?"

"A-yup," R'wn grinned at his old friend. "But I promise you it will all be worth it."

Because if R'wn had to be there at the founding of a new theology, he was damned sure intent that they would have a professional involved.

CHAPTER FOURTEEN

FAIRCHILD

FAIRCHILD WATCHED the birds and fish interact, like this pond was on *Earth* somewhere. Every version of the Hundred Acres Wood had been designed with an inward slope, to draw water back into a pond filled with *Earth* species of fish. It would eventually drain into the ground underneath, but you were guaranteed a water source for the trees and the birds, as well as all manner of things that might grow on a hostile planet.

Thrive even.

Fairchild considered that she thrived far better on hostile planets than home. Sure, being asked to give the occasional speech for a nice honorarium meant that she didn't have to work anymore, but that sort of academic life was about as yucky as living party to party had been.

Too many of her friends had started to reach burnout. A few were dead from overdoses or suicides. Others had gone white-picket-fence. More than one had found old time religion.

Something about thirty-five and *what the hell have you done with your life?* questions.

Not that she'd accomplished much. Take out accidentally discovering alien artifacts on *Escudra VI* and she was just another spoiled rich kid, finally cut off by the parental unit and forced to actually work.

Except that what she really wanted was to fly. And Fairchild was forever going to be a lucky totem to some of these superstitious academics, now that lightning had struck twice.

Montjoy was recovering some level of equilibrium. Being surrounded by all her trees and birds helped, since she had been working on the various hexagons for more than two decades now, going back to her undergraduate work.

Ann-Marta's picture was in the dictionary next to *phlegmatic*, Fairchild was sure. Calm, rational, expert.

That left Fairchild. Well, and Eleanor, but she occasionally put up comments on Fairchild's HUD about how little she wanted the limelight for this. Artificially Intelligent or not, she did not have legal standing for nearly anything in most courts. To most of those punks, she was just an exceptionally sophisticated calculator.

Fairchild knew better. Eleanor had kept her alive more than once. Not just out of jail or out of trouble, but among the living. And had been there on *Escudra VI* when the darkness had crept in the bathroom window of her mind and almost gotten control of her sanity.

Back when her Tomya Manufacturing, Ltd. Survival Tool with the high-powered signal laser might have only needed a few grams of pressure on a trigger to make it all go away.

Funny, since she got back from rescuing Dr. Odille and then trying to swim across the Styx River, she hadn't had any suicidal thoughts.

Growing up had some benefits, apparently.

"You are exceptionally quiet," Ann-Marta announced from way closer than she had been a few seconds ago.

Damned vikings always sneaking up to sack you when you weren't looking.

Fairchild held out her arms both directions as she turned to the woman.

"This is an amazing technological achievement," she said, indicating the Hundred Acres Woods that someone had actually built in place on a spaceship, carried across the galaxy, and then set down on the surface of an alien world. And growing. "What happens next?"

Ann-Marta shrugged.

"Won't be our call," she said, nodding to the side to indicate Dr. Montjoy, who was perking up and about to join the conversation. "Whoever the UN sends will eventually make that determination."

"Is there any way to extract these things intact?" Fairchild asked the boffin.

"There is not," Montjoy said glumly. "At three hundred and ninety-four meters on a facing, they were just able to excavate the right hole to put them down. And it had to be done perfectly the first time. Getting one out probably involves a massive team of workers literally knocking down all the plants and then putting everything into shuttles to fly away, if they get extreme."

"Won't work," Fairchild said sharply.

"Why not?"

She had both women's attention now. Ann-Marta had gone into that tactical/rescue mode she did when shit was on the line. Montjoy looked like she was about to stomp into a budget meeting and demand more funds from a recalcitrant department chair.

"Birds," Fairchild said. "Unless you plan on shooting them all, they will flee from people. Maybe they are already starting to nest outside the woods, but I don't remember you including anything that migrated on the seasons."

"We did not."

"Additionally, the dragons are already sneaking in and committing horticulture with strawberries," Fairchild reminded them. "Plus whatever else he hadn't told us about yet. We're already looking at cultural and ecological contamination, just from being here."

"You know, Fairchild," Montjoy laughed suddenly. "I wouldn't have ever expected to hear those words out of your mouth."

Fairchild blushed, but what else was she going to do? As she liked to remind Eleanor frequently, lazy was not equivalent to stupid. She might have dozed through most briefings, but she did absorb some of it.

Enough to use big words in the correct order even.

"She has a point, though," Ann-Marta said. "We've already had an impact. What will the UN do?"

"They would be within their rights to order us to vacate the planetary system immediately," Montjoy replied. "To order the university to send in teams to strip out everything and return the surface to as close to original condition as possible."

"Wouldn't that look like a war among the gods?" Fairchild asked.

She did NOT appreciate the way both women turned to her, jaws falling identically open as they did.

"What do you think we look like to bronze age dragons?" she asked them. "Probably close enough to gods. When a war breaks out, and that's what it will look like, are we looking at Norse *Götterdämmerung* or something from one of the more interesting Hindu Vedas? Kali-ma and the demons, perhaps? At least from the point of view of a dragon that's eighteen centimeters long?"

More silence. Shit, she'd surprised them so hard both women had to reboot.

Ann-Marta awoke first. Or whatever it was called.

"What do you propose?" she asked.

"Hell, I got no idea," Fairchild retorted. "You're a planetary surface expert and she's a planetologist. I just fly. But we need to do something. And we probably need to head back. My buddy should be returning with his friends soon."

"You really think he went to get two more dragons, to open negotiations?" Ann-Marta asked.

"Yes, why?" Fairchild asked. She went cold suddenly. "What have you done?"

At least the woman had the courtesy to look chagrined.

"The shuttle is hovering overhead, out of sight and ready to drop overnight camping gear down if we need it," Ann-Marta said.

"And?"

"And to drop down and use plasma thrusters in case we're looking at a swarm of little dragons coming here to attack us," Ann-Marta continued.

Teisha Montjoy went pale again. Gasped. Shuddered.

Fairchild just hoped her little buddy was smarter than that.

CHAPTER FIFTEEN

R'WN

R'WN STUDIED the sky from the edge of his home forest, M'nth and N'drn close by and resting on handy branches. Neither of them got enough exercise long-flying, but how many dragons really did?

He checked the packs he and M'nth had assembled. Meat. Fruit. A few tools. ALL of the mead, because he figured the professor would need a good, stiff drink when this was all done.

What did gods drink?

More questions awaiting a more complex shared language.

The sky was clear. Almost too clear. Normally, there would be a few birds out looking for an early dinner before everyone else rousted, but the gap between forests was just blue sky.

Either a sign from the old gods, or the powers of the new gods. R'wn wasn't sure. Couldn't ask the expert, either, without blowing the punchline.

"All set?" he asked.

M'nth nodded. N'drn scowled. R'wn laughed and took

87

off, two dragons falling into the wing positions that generated the best deflection for long distance flying.

Without eagles, he went a little higher than normal today. Made better time, because he wasn't zigging and zagging all the time, although this was positively sedate compared to the return flight earlier. The other two couldn't keep up at that speed.

Not many dragons could. Hopefully no eagles.

But it was lovely to just fly today, instead of constantly rotating his head to look back over his tail. They would each take a flank and all he had to do was watch the empty sky occasionally.

A dragon could get used to this, although taking the time to wipe out every stupid eagle on the planet was probably more effort than he could convince the others to provide.

The grasslands ended abruptly over there. He had returned on a different vector than a straight line home, just in case the new gods were watching and didn't already know.

That would probably mark them as people, and not gods, to be ignorant, although he wasn't sure how a professor of comparative theologies would interpret things.

They would get to find out shortly.

R'wn went high, instead of diving low under the bluefruit bush. Found a skinny branch just strong enough to hold dragons and not cats, and landed. Best to let the others have a rest, even though he wasn't breathing heavy.

They were blowing like M'nth's bellows.

"I can see you two need to get out more," R'wn teased.

"You like a long, slinky dragon?" M'nth teased back, flicking her tailtip a little to catch the eye. "One with no meat on her bones?"

N'drn harrumped with great experience and scowled mightily at the two of them.

"So here is where it gets complicated," R'wn said, turning

the conversation serious. "We're going to fly to the right and orbit around the botanical station, landing on the inner edge of the clearing where we can slip back under the thorn bush in a hurry if we have to. Clear?"

"What's waiting for us?" N'drn asked, equally serious.

"People," R'wn replied. "Maybe gods. Maybe barbarians. Certainly visitors. Intelligent. Tool-using. Language-using. Three of them when I left, all bearing the godsign."

He tapped the hieroglyph on his keelscale, the one that had come from the various warding curses left randomly around this alien hexagon. At least the magic had broken down quickly in this world.

Hisses of surprise greeted him, but R'wn was expecting that. M'nth was an inventor. She would be trying to discover new technology and how that impossible black material was fabricated.

N'drn would shortly be sharing theological controversies with the gold-skinned god.

"Ready?" he asked.

"No, but that shall not stop us," N'drn replied. "You encountered them earlier?"

R'wn nodded.

"Conversed with them?"

"Of a sort," R'wn replied. "Their voice is deeper than anything I am used to. And we do not share a spoken language. I have been drawing symbols in the dirt and the first one I met was answering the same way."

"Shit."

R'wn had to agree with M'nth on that one. Just about summed it all up.

"Three gods have visited you at your botanical station?" N'drn the professor asked, in his hard voice.

"Three visitors," R'wn corrected. "Godhead remains yet to be determined."

He stepped off the branch and fell into a glide, rather than face other questions he could not answer. All things represented risk, and this was probably the most dangerous thing he had ever done.

Second-most. Walking up to a new god and saying hello that first time still counted for all the beetles in the forest.

The three were still there: One, Two, and Three. All facing this way, so perhaps they had heard him talking to his friends. It would sound different than the alien birds that called this hexagon home.

"Oh, shit," M'nth said from behind him as she followed.

Indeed, young lady, indeed.

R'wn slid around the clearing and stalled behind his workbench. The gods had returned to the spot they had shared earlier, watching intently. He had time to see M'nth land close by and N'drn flying a wider path and landing closer to the thorns, as if the spikes would protect him from new theologies.

Long pause after the professor got himself landed. Heavy breathing.

R'wn refrained from *I told you so* at this point, but only barely. Instead, he walked around the bench, letting it provide a psychological bulwark for the other two, and addressed himself to One.

"I brought friends," he announced, as if having gods over for tea was a regular thing.

Or calling on them. Whatever.

One warbled what sounded like a cheerful reply and then leaned forward and wiped the dirt clean again. But R'wn understood that the game would require several iterations, at least until enough witnesses could be certified as sober at the time of interaction.

He was still planning on killing all the mead N'drn would leave for him and M'nth when this settled down.

One reached out a claw and drew its name in the dirt. A moment later, the god drew R'wn's name as well.

Then the stranger added a second name below his. Longer, and broken into two parts. Below that, a third name, in three parts with a line connecting two of them. One pointed at Two and introduced that god, and then did the same with Three.

Shit, this day just kept getting weirder.

R'wn heard the gasps from his co-conspirators, but there was nothing for it. He drew his name in the dirt, and then M'nth, and finally N'drn.

Just for showmanship, he bowed formally and introduced himself yet again. Next to One's name, he had put his, then M'nth's and N'drn's. It made a nice symmetry.

"M'nth, your turn," he said.

She moved with the reckless bravado of a dragon that played with liquid metal regularly, stepping close and matching his bow.

"Hiya, folks," she said. "I am M'nth the Inventor."

They both turned to N'drn now. That dragon looked like he needed a drink. But didn't they all?

"C'mon, dude," R'wn said. "I did tell you that it was too big to bring back to the nest."

"I thought you had discovered a new fruit that would have to be chopped up and dried here," the professor replied. "Not that you had opened a portal and summoned gods."

"I would have brought another botanist, N'drn," R'wn snarked at his friend. "Of course I needed the professor of comparative theologies to deal with this discovery."

For a moment, R'wn wondered if he'd pushed the dragon too far. If N'drn was about to bolt into the thorns and hide. Or punch him in the snout.

But then he'd have to admit to cowardice, after R'wn had already had conversations with the very beings that N'drn argued about. He took a deep breath, flexed his hips both ways, and waddled closer.

"Greetings, travelers from afar," he said in his best lecture voice as he bowed. "I am Professor N'drn."

One actually bowed back, head tilting forward even as it kept its torso upright in that uncomfortable kneeling pose. N'drn gasped. The other two gods did the same a moment later.

"Okay, botanist," N'drn said, his voice starting to verge over into panic at this point. "Now what?"

"I will draw your attention to the godsign each wears," R'wn replied seriously.

N'drn needed *serious* right now to ground him.

He wore the same, but only because the piece of material he and M'nth had been able to find and shape had happened to have it. Still, on his keelscales, it was almost in the same position as the three gods wore it.

Hopefully, random luck and not the start of an epic story of impossible heroics to share down the generations. R'wn didn't figure that all of his crimes should be public discussion at this point.

"What does it mean?" N'drn asked.

"I have no clue, but it is a sign from somebody," R'wn replied. "Either the Great Dragon loves us, or the trickster is playing the greatest practical joke of all time."

"So, what do they want?" M'nth asked.

CHAPTER SIXTEEN

FAIRCHILD

FAIRCHILD BOWED to her little strawberry dragon and listened to the three of them chirp and whistle at each other. Sure sounded like language to her, although she probably didn't have the right equipment to reproduce those sounds.

"Eleanor, have you been following all that?" she asked.

Next to her, both Montjoy and Ann-Marta were skittish, like a shuttle flying into a storm front that had just decided to get *weird*. That was a technical term with meteorological types. She'd heard enough of them use it, both here and on *Escudra VI*.

"I have, dear," her governess replied.

The two new dragons nearly bolted at the new voice, but Periwinkle muttered something at them and caused both to almost act sheepish.

Somewhere, a linguists professor was about to get the comm call of a lifetime. One he or she would probably still be cursing Fairchild with from her deathbed.

"Can you replicate the sound that the periwinkle dragon used to introduce himself?" Fairchild said. "It sounded the same to me, more or less, so I'm assuming his name."

Eleanor complied with a chirp that brought all five heads around, human and dragon.

Fairchild reached up and pulled Eleanor out of the pouch where she normally rode, snugly between Fairchild's breasts and least likely to be misplaced. Her case was a rectangular solid shape, about four centimeters wide by ten long, and about half a centimeter thick. There was space for a screen that almost looked like a regular comm screen, so that you could pretend to be talking to someone.

Fairchild rested Eleanor against her knee, facing out and upright enough that her front camera could watch the three dragons from about their eye level.

She reached over and added a fourth name to the human list.

"This is Eleanor," she introduced her oldest friend.

"Hello."

Periwinkle was skittish now, while the jade green dragon with black and red highlights was interested and the maroon one with some orange thrown in and the pretty blue eyes suddenly made some shimmy that reminded Fairchild of her father when he was about to dress someone down in public for some immense fuck-up too big to merely get you fired.

She studied Periwinkle for a moment. Fairchild thought his name was pretty close to *Irwin*, at least from the way he vocalized it, but for now *Periwinkle* stuck in her mind. Similarly, *EN-drin* and *OOM-noth*, but she needed to know their language and vocalizations better to get it right.

For now, she planned to call them by their main colors.

Maroon stepped closer. Not close, but the other two were both farther away.

He addressed Eleanor directly, ignoring the rest of them.

"I'm sorry, but I do not have a solid linguistic basis upon which to communicate," Eleanor explained politely to the little dragon.

Periwinkle looked up at Fairchild and she shrugged, palms up, elbows in, and whole torso moving.

She wondered how a dragon would communicate the same thought. The three dragons huddled now.

Fairchild dug into her snack pack, refreshed by Ann-Marta before joining, and pulled out three raisins and three cashews. She stayed away from the chocolate drops, unsure how they might react. Fairchild knew enough that she could poison dogs with real chocolate or grapes, but the natives seemed okay with the latter. Periwinkle had cut one up with his sword while she watched, and licked it.

She put the offerings in two piles over to one side so that she wasn't reaching towards the dragons. Next to the raisins she wrote the word in the dirt, and did the same with the cashews, just to see what they would do.

Periwinkle sniffed the raisins and studied the word. He knew what one of those was.

The cashew got the scientific approach. Periwinkle picked it up and carried it back to his workbench, like he had the banana chip earlier. Out came a smaller sword, still made of bronze, and with teeth like a saw. A chunk got laboriously hacked off and licked.

Fairchild would have laughed at that, but she'd known too many botany students and paleontologists. They licked everything, it seemed.

"Ann-Marta, what's the smallest knife you have on you?" Fairchild asked.

"Why?"

"They're using bronze, which, according to Eleanor, is fairly soft and brittle for something like this," Fairchild said. "The normal knife I carry probably weighs as much as any of them because I don't usually carry switchblades anymore."

"Usually?" Montjoy asked suddenly.

"Doc, I may look respectable these days, but that's a

pretty recent development," Fairchild grinned at her boss. "Ann-Marta can tell you some of the stupid and crazy shit I used to do."

"As long as it's past tense," Montjoy chuckled. "First Contact notwithstanding."

"Noted."

"How's this?" Ann-Marta held out a small ovaloid disk made of black plastic.

Fairchild studied it. You squeezed the sides and a blade came out of the end.

"Mind if I kill it?" she asked the woman.

"Go ahead."

Fairchild did pull out her big knife now. She'd upgraded survival knives after she'd actually needed them to survive. Took it serious enough to ask some of Ann-Marta's crazier people and bought the same one they carried.

She slipped the blade's tip into a gap and gave it a quick twist. The housing popped open like it was supposed to, so you could replace a blade from a small carton when you wore an edge down.

Fairchild figured she'd have already lost all the replacements by then, and end up having to just buy a new one anyway.

But she got it open. All three of the dragons were watching rapt, as was everyone else.

Now, the tricky part. Ah, hell, let's go for broke.

She stripped off her gloves at this point. They were thin, but not that thin. The dragons whistled and chirped as she stuffed the gloves into a pocket and got a good hold, careful not to draw blood this time.

Playing with knives was not always a safe thing, in her experience.

The blade came free and she handed Ann-Marta the

housing. One centimeter tall. About three long. Dragon skull size, if you will.

Carefully, aware of her audience, Fairchild grabbed one of the raisins and sliced it into two pieces, before resting both at the far end of the workbench and slipping the blade itself onto the wood.

Periwinkle was not the first dragon over. Jade was right on top of the blade as soon as Fairchild withdrew her hand.

She watched the little dragon pick it up in two hands and eyeball the edge like a professional. A couple of raps with knuckles. A tap against the bench.

Scientist. Tool maker, maybe?

Jade grabbed something from a pack around her belly and sliced it several times like she was using a mandoline. Happy chirps.

"What's all that?" Montjoy asked.

"So they have bronze technology," Fairchild explained. "Periwinkle has a bronze sword. He didn't exactly threaten me with it, but he carries it like you or I would when facing wolves. I'm wondering if Jade made it for him. In contrast, that blade is carbon steel with a chromium plating to keep it sharp and prevent rust, but they might not be to the Iron Age yet."

Gods, but she sounded like Eleanor now. Weird, but there were worse role models to pick from.

"You're likely to get into trouble if the UN decides we need to leave them alone and vacate the planet," Ann-Marta replied.

"I couldn't even begin to tell you how to make something like that," Fairchild retorted. "At most, it is a magic weapon from the gods or something, like all the old legends."

"Keep that in mind," Montjoy said. "It might come back to haunt you."

CHAPTER SEVENTEEN

M'NTH

M'NTH STUDIED the tool the giant had given them.

Metal, but not one she'd ever encountered before. Light, hard, sharp. Silver, but it wasn't silver when she tasted it. Had a taste more like some of the rocks to the distant, northern edge of the forest, where the mountains started to climb to their frozen peaks. Where they ran more red.

This tasted like that, but it didn't taste red.

But there was no question that it held a better edge than anything she'd ever cast and honed.

Fuckers.

Still, like R'wn, she was all about science. Just a different kind. Already, she could see mounting one like this on some sort of pole so someone could get a solid, two-handed grip and cut things with it. Or maybe permanently mount it in a housing and slice meat. Something.

And they probably had lots of this stuff.

"What are you thinking?" R'wn asked.

"Need more," M'nth replied, maybe a touch monomaniacally. "Need to figure out how they make this stuff."

"That, young lady, is usually how the most dangerous quests begin," N'drn interrupted. "Be prepared to be a hero if you go there."

"Aren't we, already?" she asked him. Asked them both. "Isn't this just another version of N'tk and the demons? The one god even has a magic necklace with a demon bound in it. They can't whistle, but the demon probably can, given time. How does that square, professor?"

For once, the man fell silent. She glanced at R'wn and caught his blink and grin that she had a witness to N'drn actually shutting up.

Not that she would tease him too mercilessly about it later. Much.

"So they're here," R'wn said. "They are at least somewhat benevolent, because they have given us samples of all sorts of foodstuffs. This most recent one is a tree nut of some sort I have never tasted. Now, they have given us a godmetal blade. What quest are they going to demand of us? What payment?"

She turned to N'drn same as R'wn did. Professor of Comparative Theologies was exactly what he was all about. R'wn had been right to bring in the big brains.

But she wanted that godmetal. Wanted the secret of it. The forging.

Oh, the tools she could craft with something that hard to work with, especially if it didn't lose an edge with use or break under twisting. She'd leaned into this one enough to have broken R'wn's sword right off and it had *flexed*.

Ductile? Hello, future inventions.

"Pretty sure I'm willing to pay whatever price they demand, if things like this are part of the deal," she told the two men. "Metal tools to dig or cut or hold? We have to get the secret of the godmetal from them, assuming they are willing to share."

"Is it a trap?" R'wn asked now.

She turned a confused snout to the dragon.

"Trap?"

He gestured around.

"New fruits that we can grow, although maybe only here," R'wn said. "Godmetal and the black material we cannot replicate. Even new gods to challenge and overthrow any existing pantheon you wanted to discuss. Could you come up with a better way to capture all of us by our curiosity and hold us?"

"He has a point," N'drn said. "Should we flee now and swear an oath to never return and never tell anyone what we have learned?"

M'nth hefted the godmetal blade and thwacked it pretty hard against R'wn's bench. Both dragons yelped at her, as did all three of the gods. Four, if you were counting the demon.

"If I could make armor out of this stuff, you could still fly pretty well, while being almost immune to eagles," she said. "What's that worth to the nest? Or digging tools that don't dull? Hell, how about making a box out of this stuff that could hold any weight and protect us from cats trying to raid the nest? They pounce and hit godmetal, then I flame him in the face? This is the freedom of our kind from predators. And the ability to start large-scale planting, if you could cut better trenches for seeds, N'drn. If it is a trap, take me right now."

Both men fell silent. She did, too, but even M'nth was a little shocked at the vehemence of her language. She'd laboriously refined bronze once they figured out how to mix the sands just right and heat it. Was there a northern red sand that she could use to make godmetal?

Her soul might be a cheap price for that kind of knowledge.

"But we have a different problem," she continued when

she realized both of the boys had gone mute. "R'wn invited me out to overnight. I thought he just wanted to fool around away from everyone, but if we intend to spend the night here, what about the gods?"

"They can fly," R'wn said. "But it is a machine that folds up around their bodies. The first one took off gloves, so I know that they are flesh underneath what we see. No scales, but maybe more like the cats that way. But it is loud when they fly. If we remained up in the leaves, we should hear them coming."

"Will they frighten away cats?" she asked.

"I have never seen one of our cats come into the hexagon," R'wn told her. "Their odd birds fly around, but always come back. I only entered here because I was so pissed off that someone had dropped this in the middle of the Trthn Meadows. Then I found the bluefruit and the strawberries, and realized that I could dry them and sell them to make money. But nobody else knows where I find them. Nor that I have moved on to committing agriculture."

"Insects?" N'drn asked.

"Strange, new forms, but generally hexapodal like us," he said. "Many new kinds of beetles, but I haven't moved up to harvesting and drying them yet. That was for the spring."

"Assuming we're still alive," M'nth said.

"Assuming, yes," R'wn agreed.

"So we intend to spend the night in a haunted forest with agents of new gods?" N'drn asked with a hard scoff in his voice. "Bully, I say!"

Shit, he'd lost his mind. The pressures had caused N'drn to snap.

"Are you crazy?" R'wn demanded before she could.

"It is a test," N'drn almost bellowed, causing everyone to jump a little. "These gods wish to see how we will react to all the things they might give us."

"And if they kill us overnight?" M'nth sasses back.

"Then we have failed, and presumably they will either annihilate the world or abandon us for another cycle of history. But we must succeed. Each of us brings skills that they have decided to test. So be it."

"So be it," M'nth answered.

She had learned how to sand-forge bronze. She would have the godmetal.

Whatever the cost.

CHAPTER EIGHTEEN

ANN-MARTA

ANN-MARTA STUDIED THE NATIVE BIYSKIANS. You didn't bring cats or dogs onto an alien world, but she'd had both in her time. Dogs were love incarnate when raised right, slobberingly happy to just hang out and do stuff with you because it was with you. Cats could be a bit more standoffish, but quite affectionate once they decided to accept your services.

These three dragons were nothing like that. Intelligent in ways that cats and dogs did not approach. Just as much personality as any she'd ever met.

Right now, they seemed to be having a most heated argument amongst themselves. The jade one slammed Fairchild's blade down once, causing the others to flinch. Then the maroon one started getting loud, but never once looked at the humans.

"What's going on?" Teisha asked.

"They're arguing about accepting gifts from gods," Fairchild spoke up before Ann-Marta could.

Both women turned to the pilot.

"They want fruit, and now have things that don't grow

here," she continued. "They work bronze, but now they understand there is such a thing as steel. Lord only knows what the big one is all about, but he seems older than the other two. And quite opinionated."

"Indeed," Ann-Marta agreed. "And I tend to second your notion of worrying about gods. How would Bronze Age barbarians on *Earth* have reacted to giants come down?"

"Not as well as these folks are doing," Teisha replied. "I wonder if they are more sophisticated than that, but haven't had the tech to exploit things. We've seen any number of larger predators around, but humans eventually hunted down the big threats at home with ranged weapons that let them kill from a safer distance. Javelin. Atlatl. Bow. Crossbow. They fly, so they might never have developed such things."

"Would a dragon-sized arrow even hurt?" Fairchild asked. "Right up there with a porcupine spine, I would think. Painful but not lethal."

"You may be right, Fairchild," Teisha replied. "Ann-Marta?"

"Nothing in the immediate area is a threat to humans," she said. "There are some animals that resemble six-limbed bobcats, but nothing as large as a cougar on any of the surveys around here. Birds that are the size of buzzards, but again, not dangerous. But we are out of scale with the ecology here."

"So we know they have language," Fairchild said. "Eleanor can maybe learn to replicate sounds, but I'm guessing none of the rest of us will be able to speak it, even if we can learn to understand."

She paused there and Ann-Marta wondered if the young woman would take that next step. Technically, Fairchild was the person responsible for First Contact, at least until Teisha Montjoy overrode and assumed command of the situation, but the doctor had not done so.

"Yes?" Teisha asked, prompting Fairchild when she didn't continue.

"Should we provide them with some sort of touchscreen device that they can draw and talk to us on?" Fairchild asked, almost cringing away as if she expected a blow, physical or verbal.

What kind of childhood had this woman had, and why had nobody intervened?

Ann-Marta didn't know many details. There was a hard line around the topics Fairchild would discuss, and she'd seen the woman stop cold in the middle of a conversation, even in the middle of a sentence, rather than reveal too much about herself. Chike might have known more, but he wasn't here to ask.

"I am reasonably confident that doing so would violate any number of the statutes around First Contact," Ann-Marta spoke up.

"I am not a lawyer," Eleanor the AI said as she suddenly reminded everyone that she was here. "Nor am I an organic lifeform with commensurate rights. However…"

Fairchild picked the AI's case up and turned her to face the humans now.

"The Treaty of Cardiff does not cover providing communication tools such as a tablet," Eleanor continued. "I'm guessing that to be an oversight on the part of the drafting bodies, to have not foreseen a species that used whistles and chirps more like a bird than human-style vocalizations. You cannot make those sounds, so would be required to rely on an AI like myself, or at least a communication computer able to handle the necessary noises. Again, I am not a lawyer, so I cannot give legal advice."

Ann-Marta smiled. The woman probably did know all those paragraphs better than anyone else. And there was a legal advisor on *Beagle*, but they hadn't reached out yet, because nobody had understood the amazing significance of what Fairchild had done.

"Dr. Montjoy?" Ann-Marta asked. "This is the point where being the project head probably requires you to have an opinion."

"Hang on," Fairchild said, gesturing.

The little, periwinkle dragon had reached under his workbench and pulled something out. A dried fruit of some sort, but the color was interesting. Bright pink.

He carried it over to middle ground, licked it once, and sat it down.

Fairchild laughed delightedly.

"Thank you," she said.

Periwinkle warbled something back.

"What was that?" Teisha asked.

"Any time I have put out fruit for him, I took a bite first, doc," Fairchild said. "To show him it was probably safe, alien aminos and trace chemicals notwithstanding. But he can handle *Earth* fruits pretty well. He just offered you what I'm guessing is a native fruit that he's been drying here on his rack, but he licked it first to say the same thing. Must be a botanist."

"Excuse me?" Teisha huffed.

"Botanists lick things," Ann-Marta interrupted. "Paleontologists are the only people worse."

Teisha turned to her for a moment, then sighed.

"I am not the one to argue that point," she said.

Ann-Marta watched Teisha reach out and carefully pick up the pink fruit. About the size of a dried blueberry, but squishier, like a raisin or cranberry. The doctor sniffed it, studied it, and yes, licked it.

"Sweet, with a hint of tartness on the back," she observed. "Rather like a blueberry that has been cross-bred for pink lemonade, but more moisture in the flesh. Should I take a bite?"

"We have a support team handy that can hot-drop in sixty seconds, Dr. Montjoy," Ann-Marta replied. "Including a former trauma surgeon. I am reasonably confident that if you have suffered no ill effects from licking it, then a bite should not be worse."

"Only serious risk is probably hallucinogenic compounds as traces that don't impact dragons," Fairchild spoke up with a grin.

Ann-Marta wondered just how much experience the woman had with such chemicals. Probably far more than the other two of them, but she doubted that was a high bar to clear.

Teisha took a nibble. Chewed carefully, but there didn't appear to be a seed. Or perhaps the dragon had already removed it for planting.

Was he intending to plant alien fruits in Earth soil to see how they grew? The place where he had apparently planted strawberry seeds lent credence to that theory.

She would mention it later.

"Indeed, more like a sweet grapefruit than lemon, but similar, perhaps splitting the difference," Teisha said after she swallowed.

The woman bowed to the periwinkle dragon.

"Thank you," she said.

He warbled something back.

"Eleanor, is he saying something like *You're welcome* each time?" Ann-Marta asked.

"The vocalizations have been remarkably similar," the AI replied. "I am willing to tentatively identify the first words in dragon we know."

"Please do," Ann-Marta said.

It would be a good sign if that was where language

lessons began, with *Please* and *Thank You* and *You're Welcome*. Humans weren't always known for such things among themselves.

She made a decision.

"I think that we should establish a camp," she announced. "Either at the center of the hex, near the water's edge, or close to here, where we have tree cover. Dr. Montjoy, with your permission, I will have my team drop the overnight pack close by via parachute."

Fairchild positively glowed with excitement, but she was already engaged in talking to her new friends, even if it would make her yet more famous back home. Teisha Montjoy made those decisions, as long as she wasn't about to be completely stoned. In which case Ann-Marta would need to evac her back to the base and a medical expert in botanical hallucinogenic compounds.

Another expert, besides Fairchild.

Teisha took a deep breath and studied the three dragons. They seemed to be just as nervous, as if they could sense the gravity of the next words spoken.

"Yes," Dr. Montjoy said. "We will spend the night here and see what our little friends do. Also, ask someone to include a tablet computer."

CHAPTER NINETEEN

R'WN

R'WN STUDIED the sky beyond the hexagon. The three new gods had walked out there after talking to a fifth being, again via the invisible waves that seemed to penetrate all things. M'nth and N'drn had joined him, but they were more hesitant.

He was right out on the edge of the leaves.

"What are you watching for?" he called to the gods, just to see if they would answer.

Interestingly, One turned to look up at him. The mouth pulled back and the eyes squinted in a manner he was beginning to associate with joy, at least from the way that god acted. The other two smiled less, but they were more serious.

The golden one even appeared to be a botanist, licking the pinkfruit and then tasting it.

Come spring, if the world had not ended in hellfire, he still planned to plant some pinkfruit seeds here in the alien realm to see if the gods would allow them to grow.

One warbled something cheerful back and pointed at the sky.

R'wn saw a dot appear. It was moving all wrong to be an eagle, as it seemed to be slowly falling from the very sky. Had some other god sent it through a portal?

One said something else, but R'wn wasn't sure what, at least until he closed up his face and began deploying wings with a wave to him that was probably universal.

Ah. The god is going to go see and inviting me to fly with it.

Fascinated, he watched the being transform by hooking various skins and deploying other things, until they returned to that original, squared-off form that had chased him into the trees this morning.

Had it only been this morning when all this started? Egads.

The sound of the god changed to the low roaring hum of flight and it took several steps before throwing itself at the sky.

R'wn could not resist. He leapt from the branch and flapped madly after the new god. One was rigidly straight. He could see where wings extended from a backpack, and at one point felt a sudden wind nearly topple him ass over teakettle when he got too close to one of the three holes— both shoulders and backpack—that were making the noise.

Ah! Some sort of machine for blowing air? Suck it in the front, push it out the back?

R'wn flew close to one arm, studying the leading edge of the god's machine wing. They understood complex aeronautics. The wing had a curve, so it would generate lift, like his own did, but they were rigid rather than flexing.

He chirped in delight at the discovery. The gods were land creatures that had conquered the sky.

What could an ambitious dragon manage?

One waggled his whole body once and then began a long, banked turn to the right, ascending in a wide cylinder intended to remain over the same general area while gaining elevation.

R'wn leaned back and flapped higher, one eye on the god and the other on the thing descending.

It fell like a seed pod. Rather than a wing, it appeared to have a giant leaf overhead that provided support, with a heavy box hanging from vines beneath it.

Not getting too close, he circled. Gossamer, like spiderwebs woven so tight that even air could not get through. It would stall extremely well in flight.

Interesting. There were more gods above, and they were dropping things from the sky.

But they were not powerful enough to simply open a portal between worlds and deliver it.

More and more, he decided that the gods were not gods, although it would be a while before he let N'drn off the hook. Now, they were looking at travelers from some incredibly distant land, come here and trying to grow things.

How far?

R'wn had never encountered an advanced life form with only four limbs. The cats and the eagles both had six, in sets of three symmetrical down the keel. Were they even of this world?

He flashed back to those rumors of lights falling from the sky around the time that the hexagon must have appeared. Five years ago, it was still meadow. Now, a perfectly-hexagonal forest had arrived.

Were they from the sky? Other stars with people?

Shit, did he need to go bribe an astronomer to get involved next? Comparative Theologies would be safe if they weren't really gods, except where the old gods had chosen not to stop the travelers.

Or were there any gods left? Best not ask N'drn that any time soon, lest the professor have a crisis of employment.

The enormous leaf seemed to exist to allow the seedpod to fall slowly, so he concentrated on it. The pod appeared to be the same black material as his armor, with the hieroglyph in gold. A grapple at the top held the whole to the falling leaf.

Something interesting. Something the travelers needed, possibly to establish a camp. That would be most educational, to watch them in their native realm.

R'wn flew another lazy circle around the falling seedpod and then dropped down to where One was circling in a wider path. No eagles dared come close with such a monster in the sky, so R'wn got to enjoy himself for once.

Usually, you needed a mob of friends at this altitude, ready to just flashfry any of those lying punks who decided to get sarky.

One's face had returned to the mirrored demon he had first met, but R'wn understood that it was just a helmet with goggles. Way better than anything M'nth could make for him, but that was a matter of technological development, not magic, he was certain.

Just for the hell of it, he turned tumbles and stalls up here, maintaining a close zone to One but not too close.

A dragon could get used to this.

CHAPTER TWENTY

FAIRCHILD

FAIRCHILD WATCHED her friend play like a porpoise with a whole set of waves. Honestly, he seemed to be having as much fun flying as she normally did. Today, she'd just taken off because she was tired of being on the ground. She hadn't really expected him to tag along, but he was approaching all of this like a scientist who also liked to surf.

The box could probably fall from this elevation, had he done something to the parachute, but the little dragon had just studied everything and then flown back to ride off her wing as they watched it land.

Almost no breeze today, and Lacumaces had turned on the targeting software, so it was going to touch down about twenty meters from Periwinkle's strawberry patch. Ann-Marta and the Doc were there, along with the other two dragons, although they were probably up in the canopy scaring birds.

Assuming you could scare a hummingbird.

Fairchild came in low and snapped up into a landing stall, detaching the leg elements and looking like an acrobat.

Periwinkle watched, warbled what might have been laughter, and did something remarkably similar.

While she collapsed everything, he watched, fascinated. But hey, he was *Advanced Bronze Age* and she'd been born on another planet.

Ann-Marta was close when the package landed and Fairchild moved in to help her corral the chute itself, folding it up into a ball and digging some straps out of a pocket to compress it into the storage bag until the jumpmaster could repack it after its return to base.

Periwinkle was close as they worked, staying out of the way but down on the ground where he didn't have a great view.

Oh, what the hell.

Fairchild opened her faceshield so she could whistle to get his attention, pointed at him when he looked over, and then tapped her left shoulder, the one closest to him, with a quick nod.

He cocked his head at her, maybe a little confused. Or concerned that she was going to bite him. She smiled and repeated the motion. He nodded. Or at least head up and down once, which they seemed to share, but still wasn't sure.

She stood up and pushed her left shoulder up and forward like a landing platform.

Finally, he warbled something and took off, circling about three meters off the deck once and then coming around behind her, flapping madly as he came in from the side now. Then he touched down.

Weighed next to nothing. Four sets of claws dug into her flight leathers, but they were bulletproof and insulated, so he wasn't going to draw blood if she didn't move suddenly.

She turned her face that way and they were almost nose to snout. He sniffed. She sniffed.

Dark flavor. Like ash or something.

Fire-breathing strawberry dragon? That might explain why he was willing to take adventurous risks with giant gods come to *Biysk*.

"Hiya," she said quietly.

He warbled something back. Sounded cheerful.

Fairchild grabbed one end of the box as Ann-Marta got the other and they carried it into the trees. Doc tagged along and Fairchild could see the other two dragons flying above, having a conversation with Periwinkle as he rode along.

After a few steps, he hopped forward and glided to a rest atop the box, letting the grooves provide him anchor points as he got carried like a pharaoh. Fairchild laughed even more at the image.

"What?" Doc asked.

"You need to walk up and see," Fairchild said. "He's riding in state today."

Montjoy came into her peripheral vision and chuckled.

"We appear to be well trained," she observed. "I've had cats like that."

That just made it all funnier. Then the other two dragons joined the first one, turning the whole thing into a flying carpet moment.

Lady Danielle Cooper, Djini. Heh.

They'd picked a spot at the center of the hexagon, near the pond. She and Ann-Marta put the box down carefully and Fairchild gestured for the kids to hop off.

They did and Ann-Marta got it open. Lacumaces had sent down three sleeping bags, a collapsing tent, and a camp kitchen box they could use to either boil water for one of the meal packs, or a battery-powered stove that would last a week.

Fairchild snagged an apple out of the bag of stuff and took a bite. Galaxy Three. Her favorite. She slipped out a pocket knife as Ann-Marta unpacked and sliced off several pieces, finding a spot for the dragons to sniff as she crossed her ankles and planted her bum on the grass.

The jade dragon approached first, sniffing and then licking while keeping up a running commentary for everyone, like the humans were following. The two other dragons noshed quickly after the first and everyone enjoyed themselves.

Except for when Ann-Marta got the tent laid out and hit it with the current that unfolded the walls and hardened them.

All three dragons disappeared as fast as their little wings could madly flap.

"You might have warned them," Doc said.

Ann-Marta gave her a put-upon, den mother kind of look.

"How, exactly, Dr. Montjoy?" the woman asked.

"Right," Doc said. "Forgetting that we're not as far along as I keep thinking. Fairchild, since you're the rebel daughter here, do you want to be responsible for explaining the tablet and how it works?"

Fairchild shuddered. Too much like her brother handing her a newborn infant niece and expecting her to carry it. Those instincts had kicked in, but she'd also made sure to get everything fixed so that it never accidentally happened to her.

But she'd found the dragons. Communicated with Periwinkle. Swapped fruit and sea stories with the little fellow. And the tablet had been her idea.

But they didn't even have technology, let alone computer sophistication. How the hell was she going to explain simple things like saving a file? Or navigating a wizard that would teach them English as a written language?

"Sure," she said, noting the instant relief on Doc's face.

And Ann-Marta.

She understood. Fairchild was a famous explorer, and

folks wouldn't be as likely to try to come down on her like a ton of bricks for crazy things. That was her persona. Doc Montjoy was supposed to be the sober and responsible adult in charge. Ann-Marta was the den mother of the planet.

That left the crazy daughter.

Fortunately, she had thirty-three years of experience in the role.

Ann-Marta handed her a simple comm. Small in her hand, just big enough to display information and watch a video if you didn't mind losing a lot of details. Still weighed more than the dragon did.

Chirps in the trees announced the imminent return of the dragons, having spooked pretty hard but relaxing now that the other two women were carrying gear inside for later. Portable, above-ground cave that deploys itself. Fairchild could see that qualifying as a magical wonder in some fairy tale.

But shit, so did most of the rest of it, if the dragons couldn't replicate something. The jade one had packed up the razor blade, so he understood, but understanding and reproducing were kilometers apart.

She chomped another bite of apple and sliced off bits for the horde to enjoy.

And maybe tempt them into meeting techno-gods.

CHAPTER TWENTY-ONE

N'DRN

N'DRN HAD a firm and solid grounding in his field. Professor of the thing, even. These creatures were not gods.

Assuming everything he had ever learned wasn't completely wrong. There was always that.

Like R'wn and M'nth, he had panicked when the thing did whatever it was doing, letting well-honed instincts for survival around dangerous creatures get him away and up. They were in the trees now.

"Anyone else feel silly?" he asked, watching two of the gods take everything that had been inside the box and putting it inside the shelter they had erected almost instantly.

"Normal for me," R'wn replied.

M'nth just grunted. But then, they all prided themselves on being forward-seeing dragons, willing to abandon the old ways when new ways proved better.

And the hoary old lizards back at the nest would be in for a life-altering shock when he introduced them to the newcomers.

"So what is it, anyway?" R'wn asked.

"A tent," M'nth replied. "They had it delivered in the big

shell. Then the one unrolled it, stepped back, and did something to cause the sides to stand up. But it's just a big leaf with a couple of poles. I'm guessing they intend to sleep there tonight. Smart if there will be dew in the morning."

"Ah, more magic, then," R'wn noted absently.

"Absolutely not," N'drn announced. "Physical properties and processes to which we are not yet privy, but *not magic*, damn it."

"Why the vehemence, oh great and growly one?" R'wn turned a sarcastic eyestalk his way.

"Magic is a thing of the gods, and thus unknowable to dragonkind," he replied, digging deep into some of the crazier arguments he had participated in, back in the undergraduate days. "They are doing things we do not understand, yes, but we can learn from them. M'nth is already slobbering at the prospect of the new godmetal. It is a made thing. That giant leaf is a made thing, as well. I will direct your attention to the color scheme and the hieroglyph. Gold on green, just as everything else is. That is a tribal distinction if I have ever encountered one."

"Huh," R'wn replied. "So I could perhaps convince the first one to make us a portable shelter light enough to carry while flying?"

"We are beetles in the foodhalls of the gods, R'wn," M'nth snarked. "Be careful what miracles you ask for."

"They have behaved," N'drn reminded both of them. "Shared food and knowledge and asked only even trade in return. And not even *even*, when you include the godmetal and the simple information that certain things are possible, because we have seen them happen."

"So now what?" she asked, but R'wn spoke before he could.

"So now we go back to the botanical station and pick up a few things," the scientist replied. "Or I do and you two remain here. We brought food sufficient. There is water handy, which might be why the travelers came to the center."

"Is it the center?" N'drn asked.

"Almost precisely," R'wn replied. "The sides are about eighteen hundred dragon-lengths each. I was counting the pacing once I saw how the two walked with the shell and had a chance to measure their impossible stride. This body of water is at the center. And water flows into it from several streams. Plus, there are weird fish."

"Interesting," N'drn noted. "That suggests that they wished things to remain softly contained in the hexagon. Perhaps this is their own botanical station? Determining what flora and fauna could survive?"

"When I feared I was facing demons, I wondered exactly that, N'drn," R'wn replied. "That they had established it as a way to feed their armies, prior to an invasion of some sort."

"Wouldn't you want it to overflow the boundaries and start taking over in that case?" M'nth asked. "Demons are supposed to be like that."

"Which is what suggests to me that they are not demons," N'drn said. "That they are conducting science, much as R'wn has, and were possibly ignorant of our kind."

"Is the world big enough for both kinds?" she countered.

"We will have to find a way to make it work," R'wn announced.

Then he hopped off the branch and flew towards the invaders. N'drn shared a look of surprised commiseration with M'nth, and they both followed.

What would a night in a demon wizard's home be like?

CHAPTER TWENTY-TWO

TEISHA

SHE WATCHED the three dragons approach, but Teisha wasn't sure where all this was headed. This planet was her project, but discovering intelligent natives probably meant that the UN would step in immediately. At best, the twelve existing hexagons would be isolated, possibly with significant walls, but she thought it more likely that they would order everything removed to return the planet as close as possible to the original state.

Teisha wondered if Fairchild's little purple dragon had already collected seeds he would sneak off with, and plant out of sight of the bureaucrats. And she certainly wasn't about to mention the knife blade that had been *lost*.

Ann-Marta pulled folding chairs from the crate and flipped them open, so Teisha settled and tried to relax.

"Fairchild, do you suppose there are more of them out there?"

Give the woman credit, she just shrugged and went back to her apple.

"Dr. Montjoy?" a voice caused her to look up. "If I may?"

Eleanor. The governess. The AI that went everywhere

with Fairchild, which was really a mark of the power and wealth of whoever the woman's family was. Teisha hadn't cared, other than confirming that people spoke extremely highly of the woman.

And everyone was a little superstitious. That would only get worse now that lightning had struck a second time.

"Fairchild, dear?" the woman asked.

Before Teisha could understand what was going on, Fairchild had pulled the AI unit out of her pocket and tossed it. Teisha caught it automatically and found herself facing the other woman directly.

Artificially Intelligent machines were supposedly highly autonomous neural nets, but Teisha had never met one with this much personality. But she supposed that Eleanor had not been programmed to handle research databases fluidly.

"Hello," Teisha said to the woman.

It really was like talking to someone on a vidcomm this way. Probably by design.

"Greetings, Doctor," Eleanor replied. "I have been digging into various archives available from the main station at central operations, and several interesting questions have come up."

"Oh?"

"While it has been generally presumed that intelligent life would be identified as such before humans landed, several philosophers have questioned that logic over the last few centuries, Dr. Montjoy," the governess explained. "They generally coalesced into a movement that presumed that we would not be able to identify such ahead of time, because we would be looking for, and I quote, *sexy space elves*, rather than understanding that intelligence didn't have to follow the same form as humans."

"I remember some such arguments from my undergrad days," Teisha replied. "Even a few sober ones."

"Just so."

"So what did they think?" Teisha asked.

Obviously, Eleanor had opinions. But the governess was also apparently concerned that she needed to remind everyone that she was not human. Had no legal standing. Couldn't be prosecuted.

"They thought that we would only recognize something after we had stumbled into it, Dr. Montjoy," Eleanor continued.

"Call me Teisha," she said.

"Teisha," Eleanor nodded. "Those scholars expected that intelligence would not be the Elder Race when it was found, because they had been at such great pains to leave no trail, and might not have, save for *Escudra VI*."

"The Sexy Space Elves theory," Teisha acknowledged.

"So they felt that we would already be shin deep in the problem," Eleanor said. "At least those of you with shins."

"And the remedy they proposed?"

"If I may be so bold, Teisha?" Eleanor paused and sidetracked. "As lead investigator, I believe that you technically qualify as planetary governor, at least as far as many of the discussions would rate such a thing."

"What changes would be implied, if that sort of thing had a legal standing?" Teisha asked.

"Several of the more prominent proponents suggested that it might be necessary to appoint a representative for the native species," Eleanor said in a quieter voice. Conspiratorial, if you would. "A human who could speak in their interests, given the presumption that they could not possibly understand the process at hand."

Teisha didn't need to look to know that Fairchild's head had come up sharply and the woman was actively glowering in this direction. It was like sunlight on Teisha's skin, even from this distance.

Still, Fairchild remained perfect silent, except to take another bite out of her apple and chew angrily in her direction.

"Indeed?" Teisha asked.

"Yes," Eleanor replied. "A Special Advocate, rather than a Special Master as some courts might appoint, but perhaps with that sort of power."

"And the purpose?"

"We can apparently communicate with the natives of *Biysk*, Governor Montjoy," the AI governess turned formal. "This is their planet, and we are visiting. Unless we intend to fully colonize it, they should be recognized with rights they do not even know they have."

Teisha nodded and blew out a heavy breath, leaning back in her chair and letting the thing hold her up.

Life, Liberty, and the Pursuit of Happiness, as it were, ***for Strawberry Dragons***.

Fairchild wasn't watching, but wasn't ignoring her, either, as the woman was enticing her three new friends with apple chunks. That was the logical implication of what Eleanor was suggesting. Appoint Fairchild as their protector, with Eleanor as an advisor, at least until the UN could appoint legal representation to argue whatever cases needed to be handled.

What would Paz Hernandez say? It had been her initial grant, twenty years ago, plus subsequent funding, that made this entire project possible, dropping twelve hexagons of *Earth* plants and materials on the surface of a foreign planet to let the plants colonize. She would have strong opinions, even as the woman was in her seventies now.

Teisha turned to Ann-Marta. Eleanor had fallen silent, but the woman didn't need to inject herself into various conversations. Ann-Marta was poised.

"As a relative outsider, what do you think?" Teisha asked her.

The Ground Services Coordinator had only been with this project for about seven months now, arriving on the same run that had brought Fairchild, but the two were not bosom buddies.

Ann-Marta studied her closely. Taking her measure, perhaps, as a person rather than just an employer.

"There are many worlds out there that are immediately habitable for humans," Ann-Marta replied after a long moment. "*Biysk* has just gone from another one on a long list, to only the second one inhabited by intelligent life, if we are all correct."

Teisha nodded and started to say something, but Ann-Marta cut her off.

"Also, if you are the planetary governor now, then the dragons are also your responsibility," she continued. "You are not the human governor, but the *planetary* one in that instance."

Shit.

Just, shit.

She hadn't even considered that.

Teisha flashed back to some of the weirder documents she had been forced to sign by the UN before she began this survey. Those included all manner of emergency declarations and powers, in the event that they were needed.

And not one of them limited her authority to the humans, frequently mentioning *all people on the surface or in the atmosphere.*

Were the dragons people?

And that, Your Honor, is the crux of the argument.

Fairchild had three dragons within reach now, each noshing on a chunk of apple and making happy sounds as they chattered amongst themselves. Many animals on *Earth* vocalized to communicate.

However, Teisha could not think of one that made armor

out of carbon-fiber plates with Spartan logos on the sides. Or cast bronze. Or made satchels and bellypacks to carry tools and food around.

Or planted strawberry seeds.

Fairchild was seated on the grass, even though there was a camp chair available. Teisha stood up and grabbed the spare chair, carrying both and walking carefully the four meters to where the action was happening and carefully taking a spot where the three dragons formed the third corner of a triangle.

Everyone was watching her now. Dragon eyes were not as mobile as a chameleon's but also not inset in the head like a human's. Stalks that let them rotate an eye individually, presumably to protect them from flying predators.

None of the bird-equivalents in the air around here could threaten a human, but the dragons would be easy prey. Like Fairchild, Teisha assumed they had unseen defenses, charged up and ready in case the humans suddenly sprang a trap.

That trap was several years old at this point, if it was a trap. Twelve enormous hexagons colonizing *Biysk*. A planetary botanical survey funded by the UN, Michigan State University, and Madame Paz Hernandez.

Governor Teisha Montjoy.

Shit.

"Fairchild?" she asked, feeling the negative energy roiling off the woman like radio waves. "I would like to ask a favor."

Fairchild's blond head turned to her in surprise.

"A favor?" she asked, blue eyes narrowing.

"If Eleanor is right, and Ann-Marta, then I have to start acting like a politician and not just a botanist," Teisha explained. "My governorship just expanded radically, and in ways completely unforeseen by the authorities back home."

"You want me to become your Special Advocate," Fairchild said flatly, rather like a child informed that they would be eating all their vegetables before they got to have dessert.

Teisha actually smiled at her. At all of them. She felt a weight slide off her back.

"Worse," she grinned.

"Worse?" Fairchild practically squirmed now.

"I want you to become their friend until we figure out what has to happen next," Teisha said. "You're likely to stop having to spend so much time adulting and go native instead."

The look of utter surprise on the woman's face was worth all the grief Teisha expected that *Beagle* would bring back.

The smile on Fairchild's face a moment later told Teisha she'd made the right choice.

Now, they just had to weather the storm of what was coming.

Good thing they had an expert in Fairchild.

CHAPTER TWENTY-THREE

FAIRCHILD

FAIRCHILD SAT THERE UTTERLY STUNNED. Gobsmacked, to quote her brother Rudy, himself something of an expert on the topic.

No more adulting? Of course that was a load of horse shit, but not flying the every three or four day loops, to pick up data because the boffins were too cheap, would be awesome. On the flipside, she'd be off base a lot more, and not around to seduce anyone. Or be seduced.

Fairchild suspected that lots more people would want to be her friend now, but only for ulterior motives having nothing to do with good sexytimes.

She automatically sliced another chunk of apple and thirded it for the gang. They seemed to like apples, but were in for a rude surprise if they tried to cultivate them.

Even Fairchild knew that you couldn't grow apples. Well, you could, but they were so chimerical that you'd get an entirely different breed if you did. Every Granny Smith apple in the galaxy was taken from a child graft of a tree originally discovered on Anne Smith's farm, centuries ago. Same with the Galaxy Three she was enjoying. Cut and graft.

Of course, alien apples raised by dragons would probably be worth their weight in platinum, if only for the story behind them.

"You got the tablet?" she asked Ann-Marta.

Rather than chuck it, the woman rose on graceful legs and walked over, handing it to her, like Fairchild could be counted on to drop it. Of course, she was really only dexterous when flying, so maybe the woman had a point.

Fairchild powered it up and put it down on the dirt in front of her, screen up. Like every bit of electronics kit, it flashed the Spartan logo before moving on to a standard touch screen.

All three of the dragons were mesmerized, like she was a snake charmer playing a mesmerical horn at them. Quickly, she navigated through screens to find the one she wanted, dropping a launch shortcut back on the main screen.

Fairchild touched that to open a painting program. The ancient one that only displayed in two dimensions, and with only a few hundred thousand color options. Black was good enough for now, but eventually she'd have to walk them through everything.

With a fingertip, she wrote her name in block capital letters across the top. Then she switched brushes, wiped everything clean, and then switched back and wrote her name again.

That started one hell of a polite argument within her petite dragon horde. Jade and maroon seemed to be ganging up on Periwinkle, possibly along the lines of *"You got us into this mess"* from the tone.

Periwinkle chirped at them, then up at her, and waddled over. He seemed to grasp that this was a touchscreen, because he leaned way out, rear legs braced and tail straight backwards as he hovered over the tablet and touched it once, dragging a clawed finger across the surface.

Thankfully, his skin composition was close enough to hers that the machine read his touch. It matched the line, and she'd set the width pretty high so that it was visible, in spite of how tiny his hands were.

It was almost like watching a light bulb come on, as he drew the same three characters from before. The one that seemed to be the two syllable name of a periwinkle dragon.

Fairchild hit save and wondered what a printout of that as a poster on some kid's wall might do to drive the next generation of boffins to dream.

She clicked NEW and they had a blank slate to work with. She added three stick figures after using the color button to make them blue. Again, periwinkle lit up.

He dove in and played with the color button until he found how hex worked and dialed it in to #CCCCFF. Fairchild leaned in and altered the width of the pencil to something finer and all of a sudden he was drawing. That same dragon he'd done in the dirt when they'd started talking, but this one looked even more like him than that had.

She watched him swap down to jade now and add a portrait of the second dragon. That one seemed more delicate, with its face blown up. Maroon seemed almost grumpy and glowering in a manner similar to Fairchild after a really bad hangover night, right before the meds kicked in to clean her system out.

Again, she showed him how to hit save. The little fellow chirped when she cleared the screen. Sounded like raw disappointment, until she clicked the OPEN button and selected the file that had just been saved, bringing it all back.

The chattering between the three dragons intensified now, as they seemed to be following along with what must look like a magic book. Jade touched the screen and added his name in a corner. Maroon seemed spellbound.

"How soon until they learn to read English, do you suppose?" a voice intruded and nearly spilled Fairchild onto her back. Good thing she was already sitting down.

Eleanor. Doc was holding her up to watch all this. Fairchild collected her and put the AI into the pocket between her breasts where she would have the best view.

"I have no idea," Fairchild replied. "We're working with people that use tools. If they grasp that this is just another tool, the stars might be the limit."

"In which case I might have a question," Ann-Marta broke in. "If they can consume the same fruits and nuts we can, does that mean that we could be exposing them to our germs? And vice versa?"

Fairchild knew a moment of pure panic that she might accidentally kill her new friends instead of protecting them.

"Everybody has had all their inoculations, right?" she asked Doc.

That woman nodded nervously.

"So maybe I need to set up something of a permanent camp outside the base and limit my interactions with people," Fairchild continued. "Just to be safe. Tomorrow, let's move the tent back to the landing zone and y'all can either drop supplies there or I won't spend a lot of time around people back at the base?"

"Do you think that is wise, Fairchild?" Doc asked.

She shrugged.

"Kinda operating without a net here, Dr. Montjoy," Fairchild said. "Excuse me, Governor Montjoy."

"You are required to call me Teisha except in formal settings, Fairchild," Doc said with a serious look on her face and a twinkle in her eyes.

"Teisha," she nodded back to the woman.

Fairchild had a hard time coming up with folks these

days that she was on a first-name basis with, not counting grad students she was seducing.

Shit, was this more adulting? Might have to go teach her new friends how to commit crop circles or something.

Can't be getting stodgy now, can we?

But Fairchild just smiled.

She turned back to the three dragons and smiled at them.

This was going to get even weirder.

PART THREE

SECOND CONTACT

CHAPTER TWENTY-FOUR

TEISHA

TEISHA WAS SITTING in her office when one of Ann-Marta's people stuck her head in the door. Andrea. Another wingsuit pilot. The one who had largely taken over flying the survey loops for Fairchild over the last six weeks.

"Dr. Montjoy," Andrea said from the threshold. "Comm room asked me to let you know that *Beagle* just arrived back i- system. Long comm lag right now, but shooting for orbit."

"Thank you," Teisha said. "Could you ask Ann-Marta to swing by?"

The woman vanished at that and Teisha put away the tablet she'd been reading. Latest survey results from eleven of the twelve hexagons, with Fairchild's entirely off-limits to anyone. No humans within twenty kilometers without prior written permission from Teisha or Ann-Marta.

One grad student was already marked for involuntary departure on the *CTSS Beagle* for testing her patience on that order.

Ann-Marta appeared quickly, taking the seat.

"You heard?" she asked.

"Andrea told me," Ann-Marta replied. "We assuming trouble?"

"We assume that everything that was theoretical yesterday becomes legally binding today, Ann-Marta," Teisha replied. "How's Fairchild doing?"

"Riding storm hammerheads," Ann-Marta laughed. "Hopefully this time she doesn't suffer a hydraulic failure forcing her to bail out in the middle of a hyper-cyclone."

Teisha nodded. That story and the storm behind it were famous now, especially with the current team on the ground here. Lightning had struck the woman twice, metaphorically, and everyone was going to try to figure out how they could be a part of whatever future mission Fairchild ended up associated with, simply because the woman was blessed by gods who had a twisted sense of humor.

"Make sure someone lets her know that we're expecting the UN to arrive shortly," Teisha said. Then she smiled. "And call a two-day holiday so you can have everyone clean everything before news crews get here and immortalize the slovenliness and graffiti."

Ann-Marta laughed. It was an inside joke, since the woman made sure that everything was clean and put away at all times, under pain of being assigned to peeling potatoes by hand for the kitchen.

But it would bring everything home to the folks on the ground. Teisha Montjoy, PhD etc., had sent back possibly the most explosive report she could have ever imagined writing. Six weeks meant that *Beagle* had been in-system at *Earth* for all of about a week, which was just barely enough time to load up on the next shipment of supplies.

Would they be carrying politicians in the sorts of genteel poverty that poor academics were forced to endure? Or would they be following along shortly in a nicer ship?

The lag just meant that everything would be handled via

text messages and emails for now, so they probably wouldn't be privy to the whole story until a shuttle arrived on the ground, bearing somebody's doom.

Maybe not doom. That was a little too harsh. But Chike Odille spent as much time talking to reporters as he did committing science. That was one of the reasons Fairchild had run off and joined the mission to *Biysk*. A closed environment that allowed no reporters.

Or hadn't.

"You'll get notes from *Beagle* on how many people will be coming down?" Teisha asked.

"I will," Ann-Marta noted soberly. "I assume that Fairchild's Grove is out of bounds, even for a flyover?"

"Fairchild's Grove?" Teisha gasped. "Is that what they're calling it now?"

"It is," Ann-Marta smiled. "More immortality for the woman who just wanted to fly."

Teisha nodded. Her own fate was likely to be more like Chike's, as long as she could navigate whatever was about to happen.

"Yes," Teisha said. "Nobody goes near it without clearing it with both of us first. Remind the pilot to come in from the north."

Ann-Marta nodded and rose, leaving Teisha alone with her fate.

Whatever was going to happen next.

CHAPTER TWENTY-FIVE

R'WN

R'WN CONTEMPLATED HIS STRAWBERRIES. He even knew the term for them now, and the vocalization. With Fairchild's help, he and the others had dug a small pond and lined it with clay, to the point that he generally had water for his crops and didn't have to rely on rain and dew.

M'nth had been a little put out, to discover that R'wn's new friend was a female, but he'd had to remind her that humans didn't mate like that or lay eggs, so she had eventually gotten mostly over herself. N'drn had brought more than one field trip of advanced students to the botanical station, in order to meet the traveler who was currently causing an existential crisis in the departments associated with Comparative Theologies.

The workbench was longer, with the addition of a chunk of something that was artificial and had once held part of Fairchild's breakfast. But it was flat and the right height. He had started drying other fruit, after Fairchild had taught him the names of things.

It was a pity that no cranberries grew here, but he'd watched a vision in the machine showing how they might be planted in a small lake. Dried, they were pretty good, but he didn't want to take up fishing for fruit.

Fairchild approached at a humor best described as stomping. It was a human thing. Dragons would fly with angry pique.

It was just the two of them today, with M'nth back at the nest trying to convince some other dragons to head north on an expedition to find the raw ingredients of the godmetal. *Iron.* Refined and purified into something WAY better than bronze.

Fairchild sat in the dirt where her bottom had worn a soft spot, and leaned back against the tree. She opened the communication machine and typed.

Typed.

The humans had stones that could be carved into letters, impressed with some sort of indelible substance, and pressed against a white leaf to store information. Once he had learned the letters and numbers, R'wn had set N'drn to having someone create a similar written dragonfont that he could use.

Dragons were mostly aural in nature, but records were kept written. Usually inscribed in fired clay.

The nest didn't know it yet, but the future was coming.

R'wn ignored his strawberries and went over to see what Fairchild had to say. Each of them could understand the other, but that was mostly emotional loading and simple sentences. They had to write for complicated things.

Boss sky ground here.

She'd used a term that generally denoted the greatest gods of a pantheon, but R'wn didn't think it was a mistake on her part. She still teased him about demons. And the humans had come from the sky. A mighty machine had delivered the hexagon when no dragons were looking and then left.

So a great personage was coming from the sky and would come here?

Well, shit.

Montjoy was a great personage, as far as Fairchild was concerned, with everyone below her in power.

Her. All three of the people he had taken for demons were females. All four, with the one demon/human who only communicated via a tiny machine and never visited in person.

Eleanor. The one who could make the right vocalizations, but she might be using the power to record sound and replay it, like this machine had.

When? R'wn asked, remembering to add the mark at the end that made it a question.

Written words probably needed tonal marks, but the humans talked differently. Maybe the two of them, with N'drn, needed to invent a whole new language, and then get M'nth to cast the letters.

R'wn. God-talker.

He wanted to giggle, but that would be inappropriate right now, as pissed off as his friend was.

Fairchild shrugged. It involved both palms up and most of the upper body. R'wn had learned to do something similar with his wings.

Two sun. Three sun. Four sun?

Ah, sometime in the next few days but she wasn't sure when.

What would that look like? It had been a month and a half, as measured by the larger moon. Had they sent a messenger to the home of the humans? Was it that far away?

R'wn decided that he wanted to see another world. M'nth would happily join him, as long as he never called it a date. N'drn would pretend to be dragged along kicking and yowling, but R'wn knew he wouldn't have to use much force.

Would any of the other dragons want to come? Most of the nest dreamed small dreams. Never flew too high nor too fast. Wouldn't leave the near vicinity of the nest itself, let alone strike out across the open fields of the Trthn Meadows to figure out what the hell had gone wrong with his maps.

Nothing had gone wrong. People had showed up and planted stuff. Some of it was even pretty tasty.

But Fairchild was on edge. She'd left her wingsuit stowed in a box today, walking about now in baggy cotton with the hieroglyph of the dangerous Michigan State University on the chest.

Bad? R'wn scrawled.

Again, the shrug.

Ah. the unknown. Yes, that was the *what-might-go-wrong?* moment, rather than *oh-shit-eagles-everywhere!*

Eagles didn't bother Fairchild. He'd taken her up to chat with one of the pissy fuckers and then flamed it full in the face when it got too curious. Dead eagle. R'wn hadn't even bothered landing and stripping meat off the corpse, just to show his disdain for the fools.

Want to fly? he asked.

Fairchild just stared at him with her snout fallen open. Shock. Good.

She blinked. Rapidly.

Not a date, he added with the mark that they had to use to indicate sarcasm.

Fairchild erupted in laughter.

A month and a half of language immersion and you get pretty good at certain things. M'nth could be a little jealous, but that just meant that she'd been willing to spend a few nights out here snuggling, as long as they paid attention to the calendar and didn't get too involved.

Now was not the time to start a family. The world was going to be a little too weird for a while. But Fairchild needed to laugh. She'd been too wound up in herself, learning to read dragon and understand his whistles, as well as helping turn a small botanical station into something that might be a farm.

"Yes," she announced, pocketing the tablet as she stood.

R'wn bounced up in the air and glided over to where the box held her wings. She stripped to skin and he was again curious about the marks in her flesh. Ink pushed deep enough to remain for years, according to her.

But she had no scales, so she could do that. He'd been trying to find a paint that he could use to do something similar on himself. It was one thing to paint up his carbon-fibre armor, but she had those marks nude.

He wanted to match her skin with his own colors, one of these days.

Quickly, the woman donned her wings. R'wn got a running start, throwing himself into the sky in pure joy and freedom. Fairchild joined him a few moments later with the demon-roar of her machines announcing the arrival of a new god in the skies.

A skin-painted, sarcastic, megadragon who was protecting the rest of her kind.

It was kinda cool, even if the skygods would be here soon to do whatever angry skygods did when you made them leave their palaces and travel great distances to interview dragons.

He knew that the human nest was in the west, a considerable flying distance away for a dragon. And while he might cheat and land on her back to rest, that was still a greater distance than he wanted to fly today.

Instead, he headed in the rough direction of the nest. They wouldn't land, but all his cousins and kin would hear her flying overhead and many of them would probably come up to see what the noise was. Too few appreciated that N'drn and his students weren't telling tall tales.

So he bugled and aimed for home, but climbed high enough to be above the trees, where pissy eagles were a risk. At least if he'd been alone.

R'wn had a friend.

CHAPTER TWENTY-SIX

FAIRCHILD

FAIRCHILD LET the sky soothe her. It was good at that. All she had ever wanted, since she had first realized the freedom it granted.

The morning was shit. She'd gotten Ann-Marta's note about *Beagle* being back. That was nearly ten days ahead of schedule, so somebody at the *Earth* end had cracked the whip pretty damned fast to score that kind of turnaround. Probably hadn't even bothered loading up on supplies, and made them return, so *Beagle* would have to stay long enough to drop bureaucrats and then head back for fresh cream and new socks.

And R'wn wanted to fly. It was like the sneaky, little trickster knew what made her tick or something. Living with a guy for six weeks will do that, but only if he's smart and paying attention.

Not too many people she'd ever met had put forth the effort. Fairchild didn't suppose she had, either, though.

So she flew.

The air was gorgeous this morning. She might see forever if she got high enough, but the thrusters on the wingsuit weren't up for that sort of thing. They were designed to get you from A to B at a relatively low altitude so you could pick up all the data dumps from the sensor units along a flight path.

And look good doing it, because this suit always showed her ass off.

Trees.

R'wn was taking them a different direction than they normally flew. Up and over a running forest that covered a lot of kilometers as it headed north towards the first rough steps of a mountain range.

"Any eagles?" she asked Eleanor on the comm.

The woman was plugged into her suit and able to use all the extra cameras simultaneously in ways that probably would have made Fairchild throw up if she tried.

"The creatures you refer to are not eagles, Fairchild," Eleanor chided her. "Even if R'wn calls them that."

"They do fill a similar ecological niche," Fairchild replied, still a little in awe at the boffin language that fell naturally from her lips these days. She was turning into a planetologist and nobody had warned her.

Or stopped her.

Harrumph. That sounded like the need to get a new tattoo, just so she didn't accidentally turn stodgy or get all white-picket-fence when she wasn't looking. Maybe she and R'wn could get something matching. There was some good enamel paint that might work on his scales, but they would need to make sure it didn't poison him.

And maybe M'nth needed to be in on it.

Fairchild had been part of more than one romantic triangle in her time, but never like this. And not any sort of poly arrangement. More just sneaking a snog and a quickie.

But the little jade dragon was a she, and a bit jealous.

Heh.

Hell, let's drag N'drn in and we'll all get matching First Contact tattoos.

The Spartan logo would probably be perfect.

"What is so funny, dear?" Eleanor asked.

Fairchild played back the conversation for her oldest friend.

"Well, we already knew you were a bit daft," Eleanor retorted, causing Fairchild to nearly lose her glide from the giggles.

Stalling and falling out of the sky would not be appropriate right now. Too many trees. And R'wn would never let her hear the end of it.

Fairchild concentrated on straight and level. Flying. Never living. Shit, no.

Just flying.

Warm sun on her bottom, open sky around her. Life was awesome.

"We have company," Eleanor said, rousing Fairchild from her meditative torpor.

Company indeed called.

Fairchild looked around and realized that the company had already surrounded her. And they were all dragons. Dozens of them, chirping and warbling as she flew past them, so she banked right and opened a wide orbit that would circle her around so everyone could get a glimpse.

Hopefully, nobody got panicky or pissed. Fairchild was pretty sure that the leathers would protect her from dragon breath, but only once before they got scorched through.

A rainbow of goofballs flew with her. Every color and secondary pattern she could imagine except tartan. Each dragon must have a primary color, but like apples they didn't necessarily look like their parents.

Fairchild reversed her orbit into a large figure eight now,

R'wn pulling tighter circles in the middle and yammering nonstop at folks.

"Their nest must be close by," Eleanor noted dryly.

"I'm guessing we more or less flew right over it in the last hundred yards," Fairchild replied. "But let's not mention that to anyone else just yet?"

"Why not?"

"R'wn has been careful not to take me to his nest, even as N'drn and the others have brought dragons to visit us, Eleanor," Fairchild said. "The other dragons are probably more frightened of us than the three intrepid explorers. Today they get to meet a god."

"Regardless of what you might tell people, Fairchild, I highly doubt your divinity," Eleanor snorted, which was impressive for a being without lungs.

So she kept flying. R'wn wasn't trying to tell her he wanted to land, so they flew a few circles and then he pointed his snout north again and indicated the direction.

She lined it up and headed off, noting that M'nth had joined them, the two little ones now drafting on her now as Fairchild's suit cut a sluice through the sky.

Head goose, as it were.

Rocks and hills ahead. Fairchild set her autopilot and rotated her head down to see what R'wn was up to. He nodded to M'nth, so she looked that way.

Jade lady was flying tense. Not angry, but resolute, maybe. R'wn warbled something and woke her up from whatever focused daydreams she'd been having and M'nth looked around.

Rather than grab for sky, M'nth started gliding down a shade, so Fairchild followed.

"What kind of rocks are these?" she asked the portable expert.

"Volcanic in nature," Eleanor answered. "Recent, but

not that recent. Several centuries old, and the weather patterns would blow most of the ash away from the dragons."

"Good to know," Fairchild said, mostly to herself.

She still wasn't sure what M'nth was up to, but she was just flying today. The best kind of therapy.

They ended up landing in a field of scree on the side of a hill, where it looked like the slope wasn't flat enough to sustain grass or trees.

Fairchild flashed back to crash-landing on *Escudra VI*, above the treeline, or whatever you wanted to call it, where only rocks and lichen grew. This place was more like Upper Switzerland, or maybe the North Cascades on the west coast of North America.

R'wn was deferring to M'nth, so Fairchild collapsed everything back into ground mode and made sure her survival tool was handy, just in case. Not as flashy or awesome as breathing fire, but she also had a WAY better range she could set things on fire if she had to.

Nobody had mentioned anything like bears or cougars in these woods, but bobcats and wolverines might get a little territorial.

Once.

M'nth and R'wn had one hell of a conversation going, so Fairchild pulled out the magic slab and set it down, in case someone wanted to ask the gods for anything. She was feeling benevolent today.

M'nth grabbed a rock and licked it, before tossing it aside and trying another.

What seek? Fairchild scrawled and knelt, putting the tablet out.

M'nth surprised her by answering, even though both of them came over to see.

Iron.

So much for cultural non-interference. Stone Age to Bronze to Iron in a single generation?

"Eleanor, we're in the right sort of place for iron, aren't we?" Fairchild asked.

"Indeed, Fairchild," the woman replied. "Is it wise to proceed?"

"We just met everyone as we flew by," Fairchild reminded her. "They seemed friendly. And the last thing we want is to turn into a cargo cult."

"True," Eleanor agreed soberly. "I suppose all knowledge truly wanted to be free, and they are already on the right path here."

"What are we looking for?"

"Pick up the tablet and I will guide you, dear," Eleanor said.

Fairchild whistled a quick *Follow me* to the others and stood up. Both dragons flapped into the air and surprised the hell out of her by each landing on a shoulder.

Now, she was a pirate with twin, fire-breathing parrots.

Not the worst way to go through life.

"A little to your left, Fairchild," Eleanor guided her.

Probably should have paid a little more attention to Chike and less to that one cute redhead.

"Okay, stop here and kneel down," Eleanor said.

Fairchild noted that things had gotten more black here. Like carbon black, when most of the soil had been a really deep brown.

A targeting reticle appeared on her Head-Up-Display, obviously put there by Eleanor.

"Grab that rock and turn it over, please," the woman said.

Oh, cool. Carbon-fibre black on top, with a weird demarcation layer of gray in the middle, and then the base of rocks were bright red. Rust red.

Rust.

Oh, shit, this was a lava field and all iron.

"Iron?" she asked, mostly to be sure.

"Correct," Eleanor said. "This volcano is more like Kīlauea, in Hawaii, in that it appears to be a shield volcano. Those tend to ooze more than explode, so you get long lava flows like this that build up."

"Can they surface mine the iron?" Fairchild asked, shocked that it might be that easy.

"Not at commercial scales, Fairchild," Eleanor replied. "But this is likely to just be M'nth and her students, so the quality and purity doesn't need to be sufficient to hand-forge a katana. At least not today."

Fairchild dropped onto her butt and held the rock up for M'nth to sniff and lick.

The squeaks of glee told her what she needed to know, so Fairchild lowered the rock and studied it.

Ran hot getting here, then cooled, and the iron settled lower than the carbon. They don't need carbon back at the nest. Well, not yet.

Let's get them industrial before we start talking oil wells and petrochemical cracking for plastics.

Fairchild gestured the dragons to stay put and flipped over several other rocks. More joy in both ears. She was on the right path, and the dragons could fly back here to get more, except that the rock in her hand weighed more than they did.

Time to invent the wheel? Maybe domesticate the equivalent of mice to haul their pumpkin to the ball?

Okay, she was just getting silly now. Sillier. Maybe. If that was possible.

"What are you planning, dear?"

"Hauling a pair of rocks back to the nest," Fairchild said. "Maybe four kilograms worth. Letting them figure out how to work it, since I suspect that iron ore like this is soft enough that bronze tools can dig out bits that M'nth can then heat up."

"I will remind you that the UN representatives are only a few days away," Eleanor said.

"Yes, and what happens if they order all of us off-planet immediately?" Fairchild shot back.

"You will have permanently altered the course of dragon civilization in the last two months," Eleanor said. "Agriculture, aquatic engineering, and now iron."

"Yup," Fairchild replied. "They will eat better, live safer, and maybe even figure out how to make cute little crossbows they can use to drive off eagles. Even if I'm not here."

"I will not ask if you think it wise," Eleanor said. "That's obvious. I'm just glad that I cannot be compelled to testify in court."

"Hey, if they wanted quiet and boring, I'm pretty sure Teisha would have found someone else to handle this gig. Personally, I think she set the UN up, but we'll never get her to admit it."

"How?"

"You think she expected me to sit quietly in a game blind and just observe our little friends?" Fairchild laughed. "Not interfere? Not *help*? Oh, sweetie, you got a lot to learn yet about humans."

"Obviously," Eleanor retorted. "I am confident, however, that you will manage to drag me along and show me in spite of my better programming. So now what?"

Fairchild grinned and turned to the kids. She opened up the kangaroo pouch and settled the rocks. Back home, had she walked into a bar with a lump like this on her belly, half a dozen fellows would have immediately left town.

She snickered and grabbed the tablet.

Carry home. Nest or hexagon?

That triggered one hell of a row between R'wn and M'nth, but she won eventually. Probably took the path of logic that the human already knew where the nest was since R'wn had flown her right over it, and that M'nth wanted the rocks for her metallurgy shop, rather than having to build a new one elsewhere. They had coal that she had been able to mine or acquire, so bronze casting was possible.

Iron really was the next step, if you had access to materials.

Little dragon caravans wending their way through the forest with pack camels about the size of Fairchild's foot. She snorted at the image.

Both dragons stopped recriminating at the sound.

Nest, please, M'nth wrote.

Fairchild nodded and pocketed the tablet.

Time to go home, and maybe raise a little hell.

CHAPTER TWENTY-SEVEN

TEISHA

DR. T. MONTJOY, PhD, Primary Investigator. Technically possibly Planetary Governor of *Biysk*.

At least she'd had time to mentally prepare herself for the shuttle that had just landed on the main pad, even if the turds were more than a week ahead of *Beagle*'s normal run schedule.

Someone was still going to catch hell if her supplies weren't loaded. All of them.

At least Ann-Marta had convinced her to start harvesting some of the fruits and vegetables growing at the various hexagons, against some moron not bringing all the food this colony needed. Colony?

Yes, colony. Humans currently residing on an already-inhabited planet. For whatever that was worth when the politicians with real power arrived.

The craft landed hard, reminding her that Fairchild wasn't the pilot over there. She always brought it down like a leaf landing. And that thing was a beast, capable of carrying forty people if you skimped on cargo.

Rather than make this an event, Teisha had just taken the

day off and joined Ann-Marta and all of her various Ground Services personnel. The messages had said not to treat this like an arrival in state, so she wasn't going to.

If they wanted to play those games, she could fall back on two decades of bureaucratic warfare in the staff budget meetings of a major university.

You people are amateurs by comparison.

But Teisha smiled. Ann-Marta smiled beside her, standing next to the transport truck for hauling people from the landing pads to the buildings.

At least the day was glorious. Air in the upper teens, so not quite warm enough to leave off the jacket. Calm with just hints of breeze occasionally. Clear skies threatening to get a little chilly tonight, but local fall was coming soon.

The landing ramp descended and hammered the rammed earth with a hard clang. That was the signal for everyone to get into vehicles and drive closer, now that the ground would be cool enough to not melt your shoes when you walked.

Teisha joined the staff and rode over. At least they treated her like another warm body, instead of someone important. She needed that to keep her grounded occasionally, so Teisha wondered if Ann-Marta had said something to her people. Ann-Marta stayed close as the others jogged up the ramp.

Three people were emerging from the shuttle as the trucks pulled alongside and people got to work cataloging the shortages that Teisha expected. She even recognized one of them, but that put a cold spot at the bottom of her stomach when she did.

Dr. Farzaneh Atefeh Jamshidi, Full Professor of Political Science, but more importantly the Provost of Michigan State University. Second only to President Ishikawa himself on the political hierarchy. Teisha's boss, up a couple of levels past her own dean and into the university administration itself.

Not a good sign, if Emerson Ishikawa had sent his right hand to *Biysk*.

The other two were men Teisha didn't know. One was older, perhaps close to her age, while the other looked like a young associate professor just awarded his PhD and settling in. Both wore modern suits that looked like they cost a significant fraction of her annual salary to tailor.

She was greeting the group in jeans and a MSU hoodie. But they had asked for a low-key arrival, so that was on them. At least her hair was pulled back in a tail and not floating into her eyes.

Farzaneh walked right up to her, perhaps subtly guiding the two men who might not have recognized their goal without dye in her hair or fancy duds.

"Teisha," she nodded amiably.

"Farzaneh," Teisha replied with a forced smile.

Just the three of them, with no lawyers or other bodyguards present, possibly not counting the taller and younger of the two men. The less pretty one. Neither man was classically handsome, but the older one had some ruggedness that went well with the mustache he sported.

They were both just utterly *pretty*.

"This is Adrien Chaplin, from the UN," Farzaneh introduced the older man. "And his assistant Fortune Noël Mathieu."

"Gentlemen," Teisha shook hands with both.

Soft hands. Paper-pushing hands rather than digging-in-mud hands. Far better manicured than Teisha had ever splurged on, even when she wanted to spoil herself.

"Dr. Montjoy," Chaplin said in English with a fluid, French accent.

Not surprising. France and Germany were the dominant nations these days, with the other founding world powers mostly empires in decline or senescence.

"This is Ann-Marta Thorgisdaughter," Teisha introduced the other woman. "She's in charge of all Ground Services Operations, so she will see you settled and taken care of while you are on the ground on *Biysk*. Her people handle support, search and rescue when needed, and security, as much as it might come up."

More hand-shaking. Ann-Marta's face betrayed no opinion on the three visitors, which said a lot, as normally the woman would be extremely affable and friendly, to put people at ease.

So she understood the stakes, as well as the players.

But then, Ann-Marta had to negotiate contracts with MSU and other schools on a regular basis.

"If you would load up," AM pointed to the truck, "I will drive us to the conference center."

It was probably not an accident that Teisha found herself seated in back with Farzaneh and Chaplin. At least the truck had a lot of space so she wasn't pushed up against the man's thigh or shoulder.

He spoke again when the vehicle was in motion.

"We understand from the reports that you are acting as Planetary Governor of *Biysk*?" Chaplin asked in a lovely voice that was probably fantastic at pillow talk.

"After consultation with my staff and Joshua Liao, my legal affairs expert aboard *Beagle*," Teisha replied calmly. "None of the contracts in place really anticipated the potential for intelligent life taking this particular form, so we had to stretch to some of the more emergency-oriented scenarios. Given the risk of certain catastrophic events being irreparable, I stepped up and established a formal colonial administration, at least until I could be more properly advised."

As in, you are advisors. This is my *planet. You may ask nicely, because I have tenure at Michigan State and not even*

*Farzaneh is likely to want to fight **that** battle in the faculty senate.*

She smiled warmly at them, especially Farzaneh. That woman smiled back, like maybe she'd already told the men this, but they hadn't listened.

Men.

"And you have isolated the human element as much as possible from the dragons?" Chaplin asked.

"With one exception, nobody is allowed inside their current reservation without prior, written permission from both myself and Ann-Marta. *Beagle* will be transporting one grad student back to *Earth* when it departs."

"And the one exception is the most famous woman in the galaxy, Dr. Montjoy," Chaplin noted.

"She is," Teisha agreed. "However, she was also the person responsible for First Contact, in all the legal and ethical complexities thereof."

"The Secretary General is not sure that Fairchild is the most…qualified person, let us say, to pursue this task," Chaplin said. He even grimaced. "Nor that the current situation is the most acceptable way to pursue the topic."

"I look forward to your suggestions and advice," Teisha nodded politely. "But it would take a great deal of effort and publicity to undo things right now. Planetary governorship brings certain powers as well as responsibilities with it. First and foremost was making sure that the dragons are protected from all outside risks and interference. We have had to institute a number of sections of the Treaty of Cardiff, especially as our little friends are currently at Class III."

Again, the grimace, like he really wanted to be friendly, but she was pushing him into using social or political force to make her give way. Probably should have chosen a different planet then.

Farzaneh was on the far side, where nobody but Teisha could see her face. That woman was almost grinning.

Class III. Metal-using civilization, after intelligent and tool-using. The mark of humanity in the two millennia or so before the Common Era. Homer, if you will, or the Yellow Emperor.

Chaplin fell silent, obviously marshaling his thoughts against the bureaucratic battle Teisha Montjoy promised.

She couldn't wait for the man to decide that his charms and *prettiness* might work on Fairchild.

CHAPTER TWENTY-EIGHT

M'NTH

M'NTH WAS BEGINNING to like this woman, even if she had to compete with her for R'wn's attention some days.

She didn't ask if he occasionally snuggled up against the woman on nights when it was just the two of them. Technically, she didn't have the right to ask for that level of exclusivity, unless she wanted to get much more serious with the dragon.

He hadn't quite forced her hand, but it was probably coming.

They were aloft, headed south again to the nest, with Fairchild hauling two enormous stones for M'nth to try to turn into godmetal. This stuff had the right taste, but was obviously oxidized all to hell, so she would need to do something to purify it in the course of casting.

Or could she convince Fairchild to tell her?

For a stranger come here to watch them and then keep them safe from other humans, Fairchild wasn't acting like a passive observer. She'd already taught them more in the past month than the nest had accumulated in the previous generation.

Was that good or evil? She needed N'drn to weigh in on that topic, as she was just a metal worker about to embark on a whole new level of awesome.

Fairchild hadn't framed it as such, but M'nth had the impression that a most polite war between the gods—the strangers—might be in the offing. Those who wanted to talk to the dragons, versus those embarrassed to admit that they had not foreseen them and now wanted everyone to leave and hide again behind the veil.

Weird.

At least nobody was suggesting the gods were coming down to punish or destroy the dragons. These gods. Back at the nest more than one apocalyptic cult had started gaining new members, convinced that the end of the world was at hand.

End of your world, maybe.

They flew. Having a big dragon in the lead made this kind of flying almost easy. M'nth just had to ride on her bow wave and flap, like those weird birds that went back and forth in the distance with the summer and winter.

"What will the elders say?" R'wn called from his wing.

"Have they forbid it?" she snapped back at him, a little irritated.

Most of the time, R'wn was the grand adventurer, but occasionally his ego needed a little coddling. Mostly on weird topics she would have never guessed.

Except that it usually had to do with other dragons. If he didn't like people, it made more sense, as he was most comfortable alone, or with just a few close friends.

"They have not," he said.

"Then they don't get to complain if it happens," M'nth reminded him. "They can forbid it later, at which point I might either haul all my stuff out to the botanical station, or see if I can get Fairchild to carry the heavy stuff north and build something at the black field."

"Is it safe?" he asked.

"I breathe fire," she reminded him. "Last time I checked you did, too."

"True."

He lapsed into silence. They flew.

A few dragons were apparently waiting in the treetops for them, because she heard the bugling as they got close to the nest, followed by a rainbow of happy lizards swarming and buzzing. Nobody got too close to Fairchild, but that wasn't unexpected. She was about nine lizards tall and weighed as much as a tree.

R'wn took the lead and flew in front of her, circling tightly to indicate where to drop. The nest wasn't in a clearing, but a stream ran through so there was a seam in the forest that made flying easier.

She nodded and stalled, which was an amazing way to fly. The engines on her suit screamed loud enough to frighten off almost everyone, but Fairchild simply dropped feet first into the darkness, while everyone else had to glide.

M'nth orbited the woman as they all settled. It looked like R'wn was putting her down in the quad of the college, which was the largest single space where she wouldn't crush anything.

School was already out for the day, from the way everyone had perched on a branch or berm to watch, students and professors, but the nest was getting a first-hand introduction to humans. And maybe gods.

When Fairchild fell silent, so did the entire forest, save for a very quiet humming from several hundred dragons. The human collapsed everything back into her usual form and opened the faceplate of her helmet, eliciting yelps and chirps, but nothing more.

M'nth found a useful rock and climbed up.

"This way, please," she yelled.

Fairchild turned to her and nodded, then walked slowly as M'nth skittered over to her forge, down by the water's edge on a slope.

M'nth marked a spot on the ground with a quick double slash and Fairchild put the two boulders here, pressing them into the soil a little so they wouldn't roll away.

M'nth didn't know what to say, and it would have required the machine to write on, unless she wanted to scrawl it in the dirt, so she flapped up and landed on Fairchild's shoulder, before leaning in and kissing the woman on the cheek.

Humans tasted salty, but not a bad taste.

Fairchild nodded and changed colors, but M'nth had never seen that shade of crimson, so she was unsure of the display. Didn't appear angry or hostile. Embarrassed, maybe?

They had to share R'wn, but M'nth got the better end of the deal because she got his snuggles, while Fairchild only had part of his mind. But that could work. The gods had obviously chosen R'wn as a new kind of prophet, bringing civilization down from the skies.

Hopefully, the price wouldn't be horrible, like in the tales of the old gods.

N'drn was already chucking out broad swathes of everything in trying to explain a new future that contained creatures doomed to only have four limbs. And the ability to travel to the stars.

Fairchild sat in an open space and R'wn hopped up on a crossed knee.

"You are nuts," he told her.

M'nth shrugged with her tail. He was a boy. He wouldn't get it, anyway.

N'drn arrived before they had to have a conversation that

might be more personal than you wanted aired before the entire nest. Fairchild pulled out the tablet and sat it in front of her where anyone could get to it.

Dozens of others, elders as well as younglings, flew close enough to witness everything like it was a poetry slam, but at the same time kept a safe and sane distance.

"Egads, but you folks like to make an entrance," N'drn announced as he emerged. "What prompted this?"

He indicated everything with both wingtips as well as his tail.

"Fairchild says that her elders from another star are coming and will be here soon," R'wn replied. "The time of decision will be upon us in the next few days."

"Is there anything we can do?" the professor asked.

"I am not sure," R'wn said. "Fairchild is despondent, so I suggested flying. We came by here because dragons cheer her up. Then we went north to the mountain and recovered boulders that might be used to forge godmetal tools."

M'nth hadn't moved more than a wingtip away from the stones as she listened, almost possessively touching them in ways she didn't want to talk about. N'drn approached now. He sniffed the stone and then licked it.

"So air will weaken it?" he asked.

Bronze would corrode eventually, but she had found an oil that would keep it mostly intact. Iron would need something similar.

"So I think," M'nth replied. "But I intend to ask Fairchild to tell us all that she is allowed to."

"Allowed?"

"The gods that come frighten her," M'nth said. "This human who is fearless. She might be taken away from us and judged. I need to learn more before she goes."

"I see," N'drn said.

She watched him walk to the tablet and power it on.

"R'wn, does she read our tongue?" he asked.

R'wn stepped close and waggled his head.

"There are some words of hers, some of ours, and a lot of spaces we have not yet covered," he said simply. "What would you ask her?"

"Can we protect her from the traveler who comes?" N'drn stated.

He never thought of them as gods, but he was a professor. M'nth was just a tinker. She left the big thoughts for the big brains.

R'wn composed a phrase and stepped back.

Boss come danger Fairchild?

M'nth looked forward to being able to talk in full sentences, rather than a babble like you might get from a hatchling. Maybe that was why the men didn't think she was a god? Shouldn't a true god be able to talk to the dragons natively?

Worms for thought.

Fairchild leaned way over, spooking about half the watchers into flight as she wrote. M'nth moved closer to see. She'd rarely encountered the written talk with the human.

Boss come danger dragons? Boss come Fairchild leave? Not know.

Huh. She was unsure what the arrival of the great one implied. But she had spent most of her time away from the humans. M'nth had quietly flown to the place where the humans had their nest, but not gotten too close. It was a loud, smelly, frightening nest.

"R'wn, ask if we should go visit the great one at the human nest instead of them coming here," M'nth said, causing both men to flinch when they looked at her. "Fairchild has been here and brought us the godmetal stone. Should we visit the hall of the gods to speak on her behalf?"

"What if she has broken their law?" N'drn asked.

"Then they aren't gods," M'nth snapped at the boffin. "They are found to just be people and we need them to be friends. If they will allow it."

She slammed her snout shut at that point, aware of how close to heresy her words had taken her. N'drn routinely thought things that she expected to get him struck down by lightning or eagles, but even the old gods had grown complacent.

If that meant a future with new gods or no gods, they needed to know the truth of it now.

R'wn gulped and wrote.

Dragons go Boss Fairchild?

M'nth could tell when the woman translated that into her own language by the gasp that came out of her snout. Fairchild and Eleanor started a conversation that spooked most of the remaining dragons into flight. Half went for overhead branches and the others moved well backwards before landing.

N'tk and her bound demon. Fairchild and her Eleanor. Uncomfortable legends made flesh and scales. The nest would never be the same.

The two humans went back and forth several times, quietly but with a great deal of emotion on both sides. The dragons watched in varying shades of awe.

M'nth had met Eleanor. Spoken with her. All of the humans were *her*, but Fairchild had said that was luck, as there were males at the main nest.

Eleanor did not frighten her. The Boss human would not frighten her.

Long flight, Fairchild wrote.

M'nth moved over and hipchecked R'wn out of the way, after giving him a quick kiss.

Have been, she wrote back. *Strange nest.*

That prompted a laugh. Fairchild seemed to relax some.

You come? Fairchild wrote.

Friends, M'nth replied.

Yes. Friends. Even if she had to share R'wn with the woman. At least for a time. The Boss might make her leave forever? Would the travelers try to hurt the dragons?

They would get flamed for their trouble, but the nest needed to be prepared, in case it needed to flee.

Fairchild turned red again. That seemed to be a good color.

Thank you, the human wrote.

M'nth nodded.

She needed to prepare N'drn to warn the nest. And she needed to learn the secrets of the godmetal forging.

Tomorrow would be here too soon.

CHAPTER TWENTY-NINE

TEISHA

TEISHA GOT everyone settled in the main conference room. This meeting was just the five of them, with Ann-Marta on her side, Farzaneh somewhere in the middle, and the two UN officials trying to look intimidating.

They were just too pretty to carry it on looks alone.

Coffee, tea, and juice. Someone had made cookies with what hopefully wasn't the last batch of dough. The room smelled like grandma's kitchen.

Anything to soften the edges on what was coming.

"Neither of them went to Ohio State, Teisha," Farzaneh said abruptly.

That just confused the men all the more, but it did mark Farzaneh as being more of an ally than Teisha might have expected.

"Old academic and sporting rivalry," Teisha explained to the men.

"I see," Chaplin began, his hands wrapped around a mug of tea. And not getting the joke in the least. "The Secretary General has sent me to more fully understand the situation.

175

We have read all of your reports several times, but there are gaps we wish to fill in."

"What gaps?" Teisha asked. "Fairchild was flying a routine sweep when she noticed a native flying nearby with a Michigan Spartans logo on his armor, which had been made from carbon-fibre plates previously marking various plantings. She subsequently managed to communicate with the little dragon. All the images her AI took were included."

"We are concerned that perhaps the humans are reading too much into animal behavior," the man replied in a tone verging on snotty as only an educated Frenchman could usually manage. "That you have anthropomorphized them more than the situation warrants."

"You think they are nothing more than performing animals, Mssr.?" Teisha asked, just to nail him in place. "Dolphins or lower primates? Is that it?"

Her voice might have grown a little sharp. All the better to draw blood, if she had to. Fairchild would be famous again, but there was a world of interest coming for her own projects, even if the UN ordered them removed from this planet. Paz would provide more funding to do this again elsewhere.

"We cannot be sure," he said carefully, backing off emotionally from the confrontation he had started.

Good cop/bad cop, except playing by yourself, as it were.

"What would convince you?" she asked. "We have evidence of agriculture. Writing. And nothing that was sent to this planet included bronze in any form. You can add tints to aluminum if you want the color, without having the weight, but you have to do that in the forging, and we did not. In short, gentlemen, I and my advisors believe that we have encountered a Class III civilization, and reacted accordingly to protect it as best we could. The United Nations is supposed to also protect them from exploitation and threat. I will presume that is why you are here. Or am I incorrect?"

The younger one flinched, but Chaplin remained calm.

"The Secretary General sent me to decide that, Dr. Montjoy," he finally said in a cold voice. "I have been empowered to investigate. And to override your declarations on the Treaty of Cardiff, if I see fit to do so. Is that sufficient?"

Well, shit. That was about the only thing Joshua had figured might trump everything. The Treaty of Cardiff could be set to one side, but only by the SecGen. Or an authorized agent.

Two pretty Frenchmen in expensive suits, perhaps?

"Understood," Teisha replied.

Not to imply acceptance. Merely that both had staked their initial positions and would begin trench warfare from there.

Being a planetary governor still brought with it a grand host of powers she could invoke, not the least of which was publicity. She made a note to inquire quietly with folks on *Beagle* if the discovery on *Biysk* had been made public yet. That would tell her everything she needed to know about how hard the French wished to play.

"So, gentlemen, would you prefer to visit Fairchild in the field, at the hexagon that has become her base of operations, or bring her here to chat?" Teisha asked.

Both had risks. Both had rewards. But Chaplin had told her in no uncertain terms that he could overrule her on most things related to the Strawberry Dragons. Not most of the rest of her authority, as that was covered under a whole different series of contracts with the UN and MSU, and those would have to be fought over either in a Michigan or Delaware Chancellery Court, depending on the incorporation papers.

"How far away is the hexagon?" Chaplin asked, smiling now like a lion given primacy over the sheep.

"Seventy kilometers by wingsuit," Teisha smiled. "Given the risks to the natives, no other aircraft or ground vehicles of any kind are allowed into that zone. In fact, your shuttle had to be rerouted to fly down outside of that when landing. So far, the only exceptions have been Ann-Marta's team airdropping supplies to Fairchild, but even then they usually get to a reasonable altitude and use directional parachutes and prevailing winds to bullseye Fairchild's landing zone."

She smiled at the men and sipped her coffee. Did they want to visit bad enough to wingsuit their way out? Farzaneh was also grinning, but it was hidden behind her mug. The two men might have been sucking lemons from the looks on their faces.

Before anyone could speak, Ann-Marta's comm chirped. The beep was enormous in the silence of the conference room.

Ann-Marta read the message, then passed the comm over to Teisha.

She looked down and wondered just how black the humor of the gods had truly gotten.

Heading your way. With company – Fairchild.

Well then.

She nodded a thank you to Ann-Marta and then sighed heavily.

"The point might already be moot, gentlemen," she announced, nodding also to Farzaneh as an ally. "Fairchild is coming here. And apparently bringing some friends."

CHAPTER THIRTY

FAIRCHILD

SHE'D STAYED up way too late answering questions from M'nth on how to extract the ore and turn it into steel. Or rather, Eleanor had explained it to her first. Eventually, Fairchild had flown home and crawled into her tent and her bag. The three ringleaders had surprised her by coming along, and even curling up inside the tent with her.

N'drn was on her chair, tucked up inside her sweatshirt. R'wn was on Fairchild's pillow above her left shoulder. M'nth, weirdest of all, had settled right on her breastbone, under the blanket but on top of her shirt, and curled up like a cat.

Her way of apologizing for being jealous? Who knew? Fairchild didn't think she'd be able to fall asleep on her back, but apparently she had, because it was morning now and she was on her left side when she opened her eyes. Two sets of dragon eyes were about ten centimeters away, bodies wrapped around each other and snuggled into a dimple on the pillow.

"Hi," she said as she stretched.

R'wn warbled something friendly. M'nth leaned over and kissed her on the end of the nose.

That was even weirder than a cat doing the same thing.

Fairchild moved slowly and carefully as she got out of her bag. The dragons had figured out the zipper on the tent pretty quickly, and she found it open along the bottom seam. Probably N'drn going out to pee in the night.

Breakfast was a fairly uncomplicated thing. In the field, a variety of vacsealed and frozen burritos of various flavors let you have different things to eat, not make a mess, and didn't take up a lot of space. This morning was chorizo and scrambled eggs, with cheese and various Mexican veggies mixed in. Comfort food, even though she wasn't badly strung out or hung over.

Her teens and twenties had left an indelible mark on her stomach.

The kids had packed food last night, so everyone sat around a small heating element and munched. Not quite a campfire, but this was an alien planet and she didn't want to accidentally set the Trthn Meadows on fire. Fairchild was in her pullover hoodie and sweatpants. The others all had their own Spartans gear now: R'wn already had and his flight armor, and then Fairchild had found a couple more plant markers and repurposed them for M'nth and N'drn.

For a college she'd never gone to, maybe she needed to demand an honorary doctorate or something, one of these days. She'd made them almost as famous as she was. R'wn was going to have his own fan club, one of these days. And the Engineering Department was going to go gaga over M'nth.

Life was good.

A sound like thunder in clear skies from the north drew her attention. It crossed over, lasting too long, so she looked up and picked out the flare as the shuttle dropped below the sound barrier finally and leveled off. Not a bad job of piloting, but not as good as she could have done.

The dragons were chittering, so she just pointed at it, wondering how good their eyes were. Just in case they missed it, she pulled the tablet and put it down.

Boss fly human nest.

They were here. Whatever that meant. Whoever they were.

Whatever was going to happen now.

We go? R'wn asked. The look on his face was almost hopeful, like he didn't want her to go alone.

Food then fly, she replied, damned if she was going to come rushing like some cute girl had just crooked a finger in Fairchild's direction.

Not that cute girls or boys couldn't get a reaction, but they needed to understand that it took more than a pretty face or nice boobs.

Most of the time.

The burrito was still gone too soon. Potty break, and it was time to wingsuit, much as she wanted to drag it out.

This was the adulting part where she had to make up for six weeks of goofing off with the dragons, as much as she had learned. And taught. All the reading she'd done to get ready for this.

They'd be making cocktail swords and buildings in no time. Plows and scythes.

Civilization, dragon style.

All three seemed to feel it in the air as she dragged out the suit and did a preflight. With Eleanor plugged in, it probably ran better now than it had fresh from the factory, so she stripped nude, got everything on and plugged in, and contemplated if she should take clothes with her.

Not worth it. Nothing she had here was clean enough to meet Important People, and she had stuff at base camp she could change into when she got there, including one snazzy suit she'd brought just because it made her ass and chest look amazing.

Girl needs that occasionally.

It was a long flight coming up. The kids would be exhausted when they got there, even flying like geese.

She whistled to get their attention, pointed at them then held up two fingers and pointed at both sides of her kangaroo pouch. A single finger and she tapped the back of her wingsuit, above the air intake.

Ride not fly? she asked on the tablet.

The chattering got animated to the point she wondered if they might Rochambeau for it. Assuming dragons knew rock, paper, scissors. She hadn't taught them.

In the end, N'drn flew right up and landed on her stomach like a rock climber. She opened the pouch and he slipped in, turning around and sticking his head out like a dog with the best window on a road trip. M'nth and R'wn both went for her shoulders, so she presumed the lovebirds were going to ride on her back, likely holding hands.

As long as nobody called it a date.

Fairchild double-checked the camp once more, since she might not be back for a few days. Everything was off, closed, or zipped up.

Should be safe.

She wondered if she was ever coming back.

PART FOUR

BUREAUCRAT

CHAPTER THIRTY-ONE

R'WN

R'WN HAD WARNED M'NTH, so they both had all twenty-four fingers gripping with wings tight against their bodies as Fairchild powered everything up with a roar and lifted off. Tails could remain twined, as they were behind the hurricane air intake and ahead of the thrusters.

If the worst happened, both of them could fly, but he understood from M'nth how long the flight was. Fairchild would do it in one go, whereas a dragon would need to rest several times. And N'drn was not a youngling anymore. Best he ride in warm comfort.

"What will happen?" M'nth asked simply as they got to level flight and Fairchild began to glide.

"They have come from a far star to decide what crimes Fairchild might have committed, and what punishments they need to levy," R'wn replied evenly.

"Will the nest suffer?" she pressed.

He shrugged, using the posture he'd picked up from Fairchild, shoulders up and hips down.

"She believes the worst will fall on her, not us," he offered. "But nobody will know until it arrives."

"She has taught us much," M'nth mused.

"And that might be her crime, in the eyes of the great ones," R'wn reminded her. "Godmetal might be only for the gods, except that we know how to begin making it now. It will take you time, but the knowledge exists and is written down, even if something happens."

"I would argue the fairness of it all," M'nth nodded, "but the gods are never fair, and these travelers might have destroyed the old gods and left us bereft."

"Don't say that too loud or N'drn might fly up here to argue with you," R'wn grinned at her.

"What replaces the gods?" she pressed on. "We have science and technology. Travelers claiming to come from far stars."

"Do we even need gods?" R'wn asked. "Or is there one set of gods that created everything, human and dragon, and then left us alone to eventually find each other? We cannot say until we meet one, and I do not think that is our destination or fate today."

"What will we meet?"

"More humans," R'wn shrugged again. "Montjoy is supposed to be a great one, but even she has elders who will want to know what the humans here found. They were not expecting dragons."

"So we must stand before god-like creatures to argue our case?" M'nth asked.

"Likely, so don't sass them too hard," R'wn grinned at her, provoking a scowl that turned into a tail hug.

"Thus we must challenge the very gods," M'nth mused. "All of them, everywhere. My mother warned me that you were going to be trouble."

"And she was right," R'wn laughed out loud. "Look at what I've gotten all of us into."

M'nth just shook her head and leaned close, sides

touching. R'wn enjoyed what he could as he watched the alien landscape ahead of them grow closer and more foreboding.

There was a wall, but it was a hollow, square mesh made of something gray, and twelve or fourteen dragons tall. His world outside it, Fairchild's inside, where machines had cut the grass to barely tall enough for a dragon to hide from a cat in.

Paths had been *made*. A black material running in straight lines or clean curves going from nest to nest. Except that those were individual caves, and the entire place was a single nest.

He could not even begin to identify most of it, except for towers in places that seemed to be pointing magical devices at the sky or nearby terrain. More eyes for Eleanor or her fellow demons to watch with.

No other fliers rose to greet them, but R'wn was not surprised. Fairchild was coming to them.

The darkest-scaled human emerged from a long, round building and waved. Ann-Marta. The Third of that original meeting that had forever changed dragonkind.

He felt Fairchild bank softly and glide towards the woman, landing sedately rather than pulling that impressive drop-stall she'd done to slip into the dragon nest yesterday. But there was space here for hundreds of dragons to be flying around at the same time.

Truly, humans feared nothing, but then, few of the animals he had ever even read about would be large enough to threaten a human. Eagles would not dare. Cats would simply run on sight.

Fairchild was getting close.

"We should drop off," he said to M'nth.

She nodded and he leapt into the air, unfurling his wings and stalling in her wake, careful not to catch her machine wind in his face, where it might topple him ass over teakettle.

M'nth made it look graceful, but she did that.

Ann-Marta laughed with joy to see them circling, and said something that sounded like a greeting.

Fairchild landed and began to turn back into a human. She said something to Ann-Marta and the woman held up her shoulder as an invitation.

R'wn landed, careful not to dig his claws in, as she was not encased in leather today, but wearing cotton in green and gold.

"Hello," he said.

She replied in a similar, cheery tone.

"Are we there yet?" an obviously-sleepy N'drn appeared from Fairchild's belly.

"Yes, you lazy dork," M'nth said as she circled. "But sit still until Fairchild is ready to deal with you. We don't want her falling over if you surprised her."

The professor grumbled but subsided.

The humans spoke briefly, and then both changed directions, walking away from the current nest towards a smaller one off to one side.

More humans, but they were all standing perfectly still with huge eyes. Their first glimpse of a dragon, and riding on Ann-Marta's shoulder. Or Fairchild's, where M'nth had landed.

"Good morning, fellow travelers," he called, prompting snorts and giggles from the other dragons.

But that was fine. The other humans recoiled and watched.

The nest was huge, even for humans. Through a tent door that was solid. Into a cave with lights. Through an opening and Fairchild lifted N'drn out and set him on a tall bed. M'nth hopped down as well, so R'wn joined them on the fluffy softness.

Fairchild stripped down to humanskin again, instead of flying leather. Humans looked weird, without scales. She had random drawing on herself, but he understood that most humans would only have a few, if any. But Fairchild was the wildchild of her nest, in ways R'wn understood.

The woman dressed in blue pants and the green hoodie with the hieroglyph on her keel. That was apparently a requirement on this world. She even put on shoes, although that was fairly rare, back at the hexagon.

But then, Fairchild wearing anything when she wasn't flying was a bit rare. Like him, she would find a good rock to stretch out and absorb the warmth of the sun. Cold season was coming.

The two humans continued talking almost constantly, but R'wn understood few of the words and none of the context. Probably just gossip, since she didn't pull out the machine to talk with dragons.

Dressed, she tapped her shoulders, but N'drn was obviously feeling lazy. He landed in her hood, while M'nth took her right shoulder.

R'wn was feeling adventurous, so he returned to Ann-Marta's shoulder and rode there. Easier than walking, and less likely to get stepped on by a giant. Plus, he expected more doors between here and wherever.

They were going to visit beings claiming to possibly be new gods, after all.

Best be prepared.

CHAPTER THIRTY-TWO

FAIRCHILD

FAIRCHILD HAD CHANGED into a pair of comfy jeans and a Spartan hoodie. Clean, which was weird, since it didn't smell like her or dragon. She'd gotten accustomed to the scent.

Gone native, as it were.

"Two of them?" she asked Ann-Marta.

"Yes," the woman replied as they started across the tarmac, organic limousines for three dragons. "Both Frenchmen. Both pretty, according to Teisha, but I would agree. Likely to play hardball. Teisha didn't know if they could actually just sweep her aside and take over the situation, but she's not feeling benevolent if they try, so it might turn into a boardroom war."

"Been through a few of those," Fairchild laughed.

Once upon a time, Father had wanted her to go into the family business. All four of her older siblings—Eva, Chloe, Junior, and Rudy—had, to some extent. But they were all kids of wives #1 and #2—Rafeela and Marina—whereas she'd been Sìleas's only. Father had gotten himself fixed after that, so Elizabeth, Paella, and Akiko didn't bear any more heirs to the fortune.

But yes, she'd been in the boardroom a few times when bodies got metaphorically piled up by her hardass sire. And she'd emailed a few things home when *Beagle* had left, to be delivered later. That might help.

"We're indoors?" Fairchild confirmed.

"That's right."

"I might suggest you have everyone in a room with an open window and no screen," Fairchild said. "The dragons might spook and I'd rather they saw an escape rather than felt they were trapped in a room with angry giants, ya know?"

"Already done, for exactly that reason," Ann-Marta laughed. "The video of that eagle getting scorched made it very clear what our friends could do if threatened."

"Thank you," Fairchild said simply.

She was responsible for them. That meant keeping them safe from the UN. Whatever those idiots thought they might be entitled to.

"Pretty, huh?" she asked, circling back to the earlier comment.

"The older one's a little more rugged," Ann-Marta said with a chuckle. "Still both might have walked right off a fashion catwalk and into the meeting."

Fairchild nodded, careful not to dislodge anyone. N'drn didn't weigh enough to strangle her, but it was weird, having his weight centered on her neck. M'nth was riding where R'wn occasionally did, but he was gracing Ann-Marta today.

Then they were at the building.

"This is the place?" she asked. "Which room?"

"First left," Ann-Marta said.

Fairchild thought about it and considered the best way to do this right. Paella, one of her stepmothers, had always told her to *make an entrance* if you wanted to own a room when you got there. She stopped and pulled out the tablet from her pouch.

Dragons circle return enter left, she typed, showing it to M'nth.

Fairchild thought she caught the draconic equivalent of a snicker from the girl-dragon, then M'nth explained it to the boys. More hooting. Possibly some laughter.

Making an entrance, dragon style.

"Ann-Marta, you hold this door open," Fairchild explained. "They are going out, swooping back, and then flying in after me, so it doesn't look like they are pets or anything. Clear?"

Human snickers this time.

"Got it."

She gestured her co-conspirators into motion and all three launched.

Fairchild took a deep breath and wondered if she had what it took to take the strangers on, head to head. She'd never been like that before, but she'd never had a cause to fight for, either. She nodded, mostly to herself, and took a deep breath.

Ann-Marta opened the door and Fairchild stepped into the admin building, turning left at the first door and confirming an open window in the far side from the door, as well as Teisha, another woman, and the two *prettyboys* in Hong Kong suits.

She'd wondered if she needed to bring out her own suit, but Teisha was in grad-student-casual and the other woman was dressed like an administrator in a dowdy blazer and skirt, so fashion would be one of the lines of demarcation between the sides.

She smiled at everyone, walked over next to Teisha, and immediately sat.

The woman started to talk, but Fairchild held up an

insistent finger to stop her, counting seconds.

The sound preceded them, but you had to have lived with a goofball dragon who occasionally liked to pounce on you when he thought you weren't paying attention.

"I brought some friends," Fairchild announced as three shapes swooped into the room, swirled madly once around like a pocket whirlwind, and then landed. R'wn, as she had expected, was on the table in front of her. N'drn was close by but nearer the edge. M'nth had landed on her shoulder again.

Girls against boys? Okay.

Fairchild let the Frenchmen settle, although the younger-looking one might have come close to peeing himself from the look on his face. She pulled the tablet and set it next to R'wn.

N'drn was the Professor of Comparative Theologies, but R'wn was the explorer. M'nth was the redneck of the three.

"Hiya, I'm Fairchild," she announced to the group.

As if anyone traveling in space might not know her name and probably her face after *Escudra VI*.

"I am Dr. Farzaneh Jamshidi," the woman introduced herself. "Provost of Michigan State University."

Oh, shit. Second-in-Command over there. Playing in the big leagues today.

"This is Ambassador Adrien Chaplin, from the UN, and his aide, Fortune Mathieu," the woman continued. "And your friends?"

"Periwinkle blue with amber and bronze highlights is R'wn," she said, pronouncing it "Irwin" like he tended to. "Maroon with some orange thrown in and the blue eyes next to him is N'drn."

EN-drin.

"Here on my shoulder is M'nth."

OOM-noth.

"I see," the lead Frenchie said. "You have named your pets?"

Oh, going to be that *kind of asshole, are we?*

But Fairchild just smiled. She'd already *made her entrance.*

Thank you, Paella.

"Not at all," she said quaintly, cocking her head like Elizabeth had done when one of the servants had let young Lady Danielle run a little too wild. As if they could have ever kept up with her anyway. "Those are the names they introduced themselves by. R'wn is the botanist. M'nth is something of a metallurgist. N'drn introduces himself as a Professor of Comparative Theologies, but I haven't really had sufficient time to explore what that means to the dragons."

Entrance.

A large rock dropped into a mud puddle makes an entrance as well. Almost as messy as what she had just done. Still, Fairchild felt better. Stronger.

None of this was anything new, to her. She just had to deal with the flashbacks to her teen years and the accompanying nightmares that would no doubt plague her for the next month or so.

Father had prepared her well. He just hadn't anticipated who she would be arguing with.

Thank you, Father.

Dr. Jamshidi had blanched at the stunt Fairchild had just pulled, but she was an academic. N'drn would be her people. If he felt like applying for a professorship somewhere.

"Hang on a moment," Fairchild said to Chaplin before everyone could recover.

She wrote the man's name phonetically on the tablet, with an arrow pointed at him and then set it down into front of R'wn.

He waddled over, studied it for a second and then look up at her. She nodded. He nodded.

"Chp'ln," he said to the man with a nod.

Dragons didn't really do vowels all that well. Still, EVERYONE else flinched hard enough that glasses of water and stuff wobbled.

Ann-Marta had made it into the room in time to see that. Fairchild heard her snicker from the corner.

Dead silence. The best kind, when someone decides to open the day by being an asshole. Not that she'd known that many men like that. Not for long, anyway.

For fun, she wiped the tablet clean and wrote Jamshidi on it, pointing now to the woman.

"Jm'shdeh," R'wn actually bowed to the woman.

The last guy got the same treatment, just because they had established the ground rules today.

"M'too."

"Thank you," she said.

R'wn said something in a friendly voice she didn't bother translating. Hopefully nobody would ask Eleanor either.

R'wn wasn't supposed to call Chaplin a pissy eagle.

Not that anyone but Ann-Marta would appreciate the reference.

"You are communicating with the dragons via written word?" Dr. Jamshidi finally managed. "They have language?"

"Yes, Dr. Jamshidi," Fairchild smiled innocently. "I can understand some of their vocalizations by now, and they mine, but complicated things require a sort of pidgin vernacular we have been working out phonetically over the last six weeks."

R'wn wiped the tablet clean now and wrote something, sliding it around to her to read.

M'nth growled in her ear, but only loud enough that Fairchild might hear it.

Boss?

Fairchild looked up and let her face grow serious.

"R'wn would like to know where you fall in the political scheme of things, Dr. Jamshidi," she said simply.

"What did he write?" the woman demanded.

Fairchild slid it around and watched the three strangers study the word.

"What does it mean?" Chaplin also demanded.

"The word translates as *Boss*," Fairchild said. "The implication is Dr. Montjoy's superiors. I told them bosses were coming from off-world. He understands Mr. Chaplin to be a powerful outsider, but is confirming your position, Dr. Jamshidi, as I had written you down with a mark meaning professor."

More dead silence.

Thank you so very much, Father, for all those lessons on power politics and boardroom intrigue.

On top of that, it wasn't like she hadn't spent the last six weeks planning this stunt, or anything silly like that. Or the last couple of years being famous and understanding how to work *that* machine to your advantage when pissy eagles thought they had a more important opinion.

The UN might think they were the shit, but the former Lady Danielle Cooper knew a thing or two about power. And could still call one of Father's house attorneys and get the man to gnaw off some bureaucrat's leg if she asked nice enough. Or if the social and political risk to Father appeared sufficient.

Right this moment, the Provost woman needed to pick sides, regardless of what she thought she could have gotten away with this morning.

"I represent the University," the woman temporized carefully, not letting Fairchild draw her into a trap like she'd already done with the others.

Eleanor might not be allowed to testify in court, but that wasn't about to stop the woman video-taping all of this from her pocket between Fairchild's breasts. She wondered if the three of them even realized Fairchild had her AI handy.

How much preparation did you do into my background, boys?

Fairchild had legally changed her name. Made it easier to not have checks made out to Lady Cooper. Or to explain *that* to strangers.

And Father's attorneys were angry piranha when it came to protecting Alphonse Cooper, Sr., so they would extend that to anyone snooping around the man's youngest daughter.

Oh yes, I know boardroom intrigue. Teisha might have been ill-prepared, but she's never been famous.

So Fairchild smiled. Reached out and erased the question mark and added an exclamation point instead.

R'wn nodded sagely and said something a little more polite to everyone this time.

At least the dragon was certain that the strangers really were just people, and not gods. N'drn might have his doubts, but not R'wn.

A rude thought could not be contained, and the visitors were still off-keel, so Fairchild wiped the tablet and wrote Professor Jamshidi again, before sliding it over to N'drn.

He read it. Asked R'wn something. Looked at her and Teisha. Fairchild nodded.

Then N'drn waddled over to Jamshidi's zone of the oval conference table and plopped down.

"Greetings," he said gravely. And bowed.

Fairchild translated.

"N'drn is treating you like a fellow professor," Fairchild explained. "What did you teach before you went into administration?"

"Political Science," the woman answered automatically,

but Fairchild wasn't sure that there was anybody home behind those big eyes right now.

"There you go," she said, as if that would explain everything.

Whatever these fools had expected, they hadn't gotten it.

You can order me off the planet, but you better not hurt my friends in the process, bubbles.

Fairchild smiled. Teisha was doing a pretty good job of keeping a stern face in her role as Planetary Governor. Ann-Marta had a grin that might light up a room.

She turned to the prettyboys and let herself look innocent. Fairchild had a lot of experience at that sort of thing, too.

"So what questions can I or my friends answer for you?" Fairchild asked, letting the temperature of the room drift back something closer to normal.

An entrance is important, but then the party must be allowed to unfold normally. Again, Paella knew her shit and had taught a young step-daughter things Alphonse would have never understood.

Pretty French boy finally found his balance again. Might make a pretty good dancer, but he certainly wouldn't ever be her type.

Never date a man prettier than you are. Her stepmother Akiko this time, but still utterly sage advice. But then, Alphonse had liked smart, beautiful women, rather than bimbos with big chests. That he couldn't keep them around long said more about him than them, and Fairchild had spoken with all six of her mothers in the last two years.

"Your reports of *Biysk* claim that the dragons are a Class III civilization under the Treaty of Cardiff," Chaplin said simply.

"That's right," Fairchild replied. "Bronze working when I made First Contact. Would you like some examples?"

Gasps.

Seriously? You people are amateurs. Or bull-headed dumbasses, take your pick.

She waited. Eleanor had recorded it all.

Did you people think this was all an elaborate scheme because I LIKED publicity?

Morons.

"Yes, that would be wonderful," Chaplin eventually managed in a ragged voice.

Fairchild didn't think that the man was being sarcastic. Like Jamshidi, his brain had rebooted or something and he was on verbal autopilot until some future moment when everything came back together.

She turned her head to look at M'nth now and smiled. The dragon returned it with a friendly chirp.

"Bronze tools?" she asked carefully, using the English vocalizations.

M'nth nodded again and grabbed sky, swooping just a bit before she stalled and landed like a parachute next to R'wn.

"Sit still," the dragon told her sort-of boyfriend, and then grabbed the sword off his baldric and pulled it free.

Still about two olives worth. Fairchild was hoping to swap for it and keep the thing as a memento when this was all done and M'nth was making little dragon katanas for everyone.

Like a knight approaching her king, M'nth held the little sword with one hand and draped the blade across her other arm.

Dragons skittered on four limbs quickly, but waddled on two, the tail getting in the way. M'nth waddled, but made it look graceful as she approached and held out the sword to Chaplin.

"Take it carefully," Fairchild told the man.

He paused, looking like a man expecting a teacup Chihuahua to leap up and maul him.

"Is it dangerous?" he asked as he reached out.

"She," Fairchild said.

"What?"

"M'nth is a female dragon," Fairchild smiled. "The other two are males. And no, she's not dangerous if you act polite."

She wondered how the man would react, but he held out his hand palm up and M'nth laid the blade flat, nodded, and waddled back to where R'wn was sitting.

Chaplin studied the two-centimeter-long sword, Mathieu leaning close on one side and Jamshidi on the other.

"Is that the one he had before?" Teisha asked.

"It is," Fairchild replied. "M'nth is planning on making him something better, but we've been pursuing other projects right now."

"Such as?" Chaplin suddenly perked up. "What have you been teaching these creatures?"

"I have been teaching my friends better agriculture techniques," Fairchild let her voice get nasty. "R'wn was already harvesting wild strawberries and blueberries in order to dry the fruit. He had moved up to planting seeds, so we've done a few bits of aquatic engineering by digging a small pond then adding some canals so that he could water without having to carry buckets. They aren't really fans of most varietals of grapes, but might dry them for trade to other nests. R'wn informed me that cranberries, as much as he enjoyed the taste, sounded like a pain in the tail and asked if we could just trade for dried ones. That sort of thing."

She couldn't help the way she'd leaned forward, palms flat. Both R'wn and M'nth had picked up her energy and seemed to be sizing the humans up as eagles, so she drew a loud breath and leaned back.

M'nth took off, circled once, and landed on her shoulder before adding a kiss on her cheek.

What was it with the dragon? Or was it her wingmate sister understanding the situation?

Weirder shit had happened in her life.

Barely.

R'wn grabbed the tablet and pushed it across the table towards Chaplin, noisy enough that everything stopped as people watched. He wiped the screen and wrote something, turning it around for the human to read.

Fairchild decided to be a shit. She got up herself carefully and walked around the table so she and M'nth could lurk above the man. Men tended to do it to women as a power thing. Turnabout was only fair.

Boss next???

Oh wow. You've pissed off a strawberry dragon.

"He's inquiring who your boss is, Mssr. Chaplin," Fairchild said. "Three question marks here indicate levels, rather than intensity of thought, so he wants to know who is the top human in your nest. Think how Mandarin uses the term *ten thousand* to indicate *everything*."

The man was even wearing a pretty cologne, from this close. Too sweet to be the sort of musk on a lumberjack that might set her tongue to wagging. Thankfully, it was also so subtle that she hadn't picked it up from the other side of the table.

"I report directly to the Secretary General, Madame Fairchild," he said sternly.

Fairchild nodded and leaned across the man, between the two actually, without touching her chest to Chaplin's shoulder. She wiped the tablet and scrawled on it, then returned to her side and plopped down.

Skygod -1.

"What does that mean?"

"Skygod is their chief deity," Fairchild said. "At least according to N'drn. Since humans don't have a similar theology going on, we've co-opted the term to talk about human culture. Here it means that the SecGen is Skygod, and one level above you. Thus, you are important people."

"Yes," he agreed. "I am. You would do well to remember that."

He'd been pushing, so Fairchild decided to play her first big trump card on the asshole. Everything up until now was really just foreplay as far as she was concerned. Things Alphonse had taught her, as had all six of her mothers. And late nights reading legal documents getting ready for this.

She'd just hoped to never have to use the stuff she'd been forced to learn. Like maybe she could have walked in here and plopped down with some xenobiologist nerds to tell them all the neat shit she'd done in the last two months.

Apparently not.

"Oh, yes," she smiled at the man. "And I am the dragon's Ambassador to the United Nations, Ambassador Chaplin."

Mud puddle. Big rock. Bigger splash.

But Fairchild had thirty-three years' experience at rising from the mud and still smelling like a rose.

Pretty boy over there wasn't likely to be so lucky.

CHAPTER THIRTY-THREE

N'DRN

N'DRN NOTED the body language and vocalizations between the humans, largely ignoring the quiet commentary between M'nth and R'wn. This was not a sporting event, however much those two were treating it.

The two males were punks. He was a professor, so he could make that an official opinion. And he would when the elders asked later. The female was also a professor, but a leaf-pusher rather than an educator, from the signs Fairchild had written.

He wondered if anyone understood just how much she had been writing down during this conversation and not saying out loud.

Tempers were right on the verge of exploding. Fairchild had apparently pushed this hard on purpose, but N'drn wasn't entirely sure why, other than she was apparently one dragon against three to five eagles right now.

Probably an even fight, knowing Fairchild.

But she'd brought friends.

Everyone had somehow forgotten that.

N'drn decided the time had come to deal with the overabundance of pomposity around him.

After all, if anyone was going to be a pompous ass here, it was going to start with him.

The rest of you fuckers are junior varsity anyway.

He waddled sedately over to the tablet, the sound of his rear claws on the surface just noisy enough to draw eyes and attention. Everything fell to silence as he grabbed the device and dragged it back to the female professor.

It made a bit of a clatter when he slammed it down, but that was on purpose and he already knew it could fall at least five dragonlengths onto stone and not rupture.

And that had been M'nth's fault.

Still, the woman had stopped breathing. For humans, that was a sign of stress. At least according to Fairchild.

Bully!

He wiped it clean and wrote the woman a message, without all the subtext Fairchild and R'wn had been using.

Professor? Of?

He sat back and smiled at the woman innocently. She didn't belong to the two males by culture or social grouping. Might as well cut her out now like herding a beetle.

N'drn also wondered how long it would take all the humans to learn dragon language in the written form. Or if they'd thought to bring a linguist with them from the stars.

Fairchild had a low to medium opinion of bureaucrats and college administrators. As an expert on that topic, N'drn really couldn't dispute the woman.

But he needed this one. They all needed her, humans and dragons alike, even if most of them were ignorant fools right now.

Fairchild read the words and then spoke to the new female.

Beetle, successfully cut from the herd and driven off for

slaughter. Except he didn't need to eat her. Just get her on his side of the debate.

Fairchild leaned over and scrawled on the tablet, then had the female trace the letters below.

Ah, so she's onto my game. Good. The rest of you juveniles could learn something from this woman.

Interesting. Professor of politics? What a silly thing. But then, humans were silly people. Must come of all that mass. You reach a point where the nest can no longer assemble to govern, so they must appoint experts.

Sounded like a dumb way to put the criminals in charge. Especially if you passed laws supporting them.

He added his full title below hers, using the same first word, as they were both professors. If she was just a bureaucrat these days, that was a personal failing.

He could still cut a swath through the student body, opening up little minds to the breadth of logic and beauty in the world.

More human vocalizations between the women. He caught his name, but that was just Fairchild explaining things for the small-minded over there.

Leaf-pushers, the lot of them.

Still, utter distraction complete. And Fairchild was innocent of whatever she had been doing, because obviously the three dragons were all opinionated shits themselves. In that, he would grant equality to R'wn and M'nth.

And now sounded like a lovely time to screw with everyone's day. The sun was near zenith. This was the traditional median for food back at the nest, before you settled your load for the second half.

Lunch? he scrawled on the tablet below everything else.

"What are you up to now, you old fart?" M'nth called from her perch.

"It behooves at least one of us to pretend to some level of

civility, young lady," he countered. "I suggested lunch to Fairchild. I appreciate that we all had a late breakfast, but they don't need to know that. And this might be a long afternoon, as the visitors do not appear to have prepared their homework, nor studied for a pop quiz. We should take advantage of that. Fairchild already seems prepared."

Fairchild looked at him.

"Hungry?" she asked out loud, even a bit curious.

"No," he smiled at her. "But midday."

He had to remember not to get complicated when talking out loud to her.

Not yet, anyway. Give the woman a year and she might be teaching classes at the college with him.

She nodded in apparent understanding and spoke to the humans. From the reaction, you might have thought that someone had just yelled "BOBCAT!" at the top of their lungs.

Why Fairchild wanted the other humans so off-keel wasn't clear, but he could play.

TEISHA HADN'T BEEN MENTALLY prepared for today, and she actually knew Fairchild to some extent. Not as well as Ann-Marta, but far better than the two pretty Frenchmen.

She had not been ready for the show the four dragons had put on. Yes, four. Fairchild was fully native now, in the ways of the best sociologists. She could talk to the dragons, but more importantly, she could communicate with them at a social and cultural level.

Teisha didn't read dragon yet, but she suspected that the group was communicating far more than the simple phrases spoken aloud. And the little professor was up to something. Thus, it behooved her as Planetary Governor to keep things as formal as necessary while everyone worked out exactly what First Contact *implied*.

So she had agreed to break for lunch and informed the kitchen crew to turn the heat up on everything.

Nothing fancy or elegant. It all had to be hauled across the stars from home, so if the UN officials wanted to complain about eating from communal troughs with the rest of her staff, they had better have brought all her food supplies with them on *Beagle*, hadn't they?

Ann-Marta had not given her the full report from *Beagle* on the supplies this ship had carried back yet, so Teisha suspected that the news would be bad. Not catastrophic enough to derail the meeting with Fairchild, but not so irrelevant that Ann-Marta could lean in and tell her not to worry.

Now, Teisha led everyone over to the kitchen. She had developed a much greater appreciation of Ann-Marta when that woman brought her own cooks with the Ground Services contract and replaced the folks that Teisha had been employing. Amateur line cooks versus chefs, more or less.

Rank allowed Teisha to be first through the line, with a dragon perched on her shoulder. R'wn, who had been First Contact and was a botanist like her. Or how she was when she was being a scientist and not an administrator.

Fairchild was next, with M'nth, the female. Professor N'drn rode on Ann-Marta's shoulder, followed by Farzaneh then the two Frenchmen.

The room had already fallen to silence when she walked in and everyone saw R'wn. He, of course, had to greet the entire room, but Fairchild had warned her that it was coming.

The young man on the other side of the food line with the metal spoon in his hand seemed to have forgotten how to breathe.

"I'll have the baked ziti with two meatballs," she said to him, louder than strictly necessary, but enough to break him out of his trance.

Normally, she'd only get one, as they were large, but apparently the dragons had a thing for Italian spices and Fairchild had suggested that all three of them might share part of one. It might weigh as much as any of them.

She was holding her tray as she got the pasta and slid down to get salad next. R'wn glided right off her shoulder to the counter, eliciting a brief shriek from the woman refilling salad toppings. He didn't touch anything, just sniffed.

"Is that a dragon?" the woman whispered.

"His name is R'wn," Teisha replied, like it was the most normal thing in the world.

Considering her day so far, it might be.

Fairchild rescued everyone by reaching out and pointing things out as nuts, fruit, meat, and topping in a loud, clear voice.

R'wn wanted sunflower seeds, so Teisha got a small dish and scooped some in. And a crouton. Just one.

Fairchild had gone for the chicken parmigiana and fettuccine alfredo. She also got a salad, but did everything in individual serving cups and listened to M'nth chirp as she loaded up.

Not to be outdone, N'drn warbled something and gestured at all of it inclusively like a Roman Emperor, so Ann-Marta got each of them a bowl of salad.

Weird. At least the UN representatives were behaving as if this wasn't a complete circus, although anyone could turn it into one quickly enough with a little pushing. Teisha had been concerned that Fairchild was going to, but N'drn had derailed everything rather masterfully, if she looked at him as a fussy, little dean in charge of his fiefdom.

Professor of Comparative Theologies actually made sense to her that way, if you crossed a Christian divinities program with a Buddhist monk who had a sense of humor.

The group ended up at a long trestle table, with Fairchild making a point to sit next to Chaplin, rather than across from him or avoiding him. All three of the dragons had ended up on the table, sampling various things and keeping up a running commentary.

The place was much quieter than normal today.

"So what is the UN really up to, Ambassador?" Fairchild asked in a voice that sounded polite and friendly, as opposed to earlier, when she'd come in hard and stubborn.

But no one had ever accused that woman of being dumb. Immature and sensual, but never dumb. You just had to fly with her once to understand that.

"Dr. Montjoy sent in a report that humans had made First Contact with a previously unrecognized intelligent species on *Biysk*, Madame," he replied around his pasta. "That caused a great deal of consternation. Her images of dragons smaller than birds left many questioning her conclusions."

Teisha caught the glance in her direction. Not an apology, but certainly perhaps a recognition that they might have fucked that one up. N'drn and the others had gone beyond anything you might train a dog in a short time.

"If it hadn't been for a Spartans logo on R'wn's shoulder, I would have never considered it, Mssr. Chaplin," she replied carefully. "From there, it was luck on everyone's part. I'm sure you've read the report of me trading trail mix for dried blueberries with R'wn. When I brought in Dr. Montjoy and Ann-Marta, he returned with M'nth and N'drn. For the last six weeks, I have been occasionally commuting to base to pick up clean laundry, bathing in the pond, and getting supplies air-dropped to me out in the field."

"I see," he said. "And teaching them language."

"Teaching them a new language," Fairchild corrected him. "They already had a written tongue. I wrote my name. R'wn wrote his. Everything since then has been finding common ground."

"And what do you think should happen next?" the man asked, suddenly a UN bureaucrat again and not a slightly-overwhelmed fashion model.

Teisha saw the transformation, but she wasn't sure that Fairchild or the others had.

All three of the dragons had looked up, but she supposed that they had to study body language as much as words, with so little in common.

Fairchild paused to take a bite of her chicken, offering M'nth a sliver when that woman chirped inquisitively. Then she put down her silverware.

"The dragons didn't know anything else existed," she said. "They have only rarely flown more than twenty kilometers in any single direction. Partly, that's the relative size of predators around here, but partly this nest has everything they needed within close proximity."

"*This* nest?" the man confirmed.

"This one," Fairchild nodded. "N'drn has had students from other nests, but I'm not sure if I have ever met an outsider yet. However, this nest only numbers in the hundreds, so I expect that once we start looking, we will find others. Perhaps once our friends put out the word, diplomat dragons will start traveling to visit us."

The man recoiled, ever so slightly. Fairchild nodded.

"What are the UN's plans for this planet?" she asked, lancing straight to the man's heart from the way he blinked in surprise. "A new Eden?"

Silence. Awkwardly long, at that.

Teisha sliced off slivers of meatball and put them within easy dragon-reach as she listened to the way the people around her were breathing. Dragons included.

"*Biysk* is perhaps the most *Earth*-like planet we have yet encountered," Chaplin finally said. "Yes, there are dozens of others that the Elder Race terraformed into places where we might live, but none so closely replicated our home."

"And it being previously occupied messes with somebody's plans to get rich," Fairchild nodded.

Both Chaplin and Mathieu snapped around to stare at her.

"Do you own stock in a colonial charter corporation with their eyes on *Biysk*, Ambassador?" she pressed. "Is that why you're here?"

Teisha drew a breath to interrupt this conversation before things got ugly but Ann-Marta reached out and tapped her on the shin with a foot before she opened her mouth.

Teisha looked at the woman across from her and noted the quiet shake of the head.

But Fairchild was about to get herself in the crosshairs of senior and powerful UN bureaucrats. Even Farzaneh had fallen silent.

What did Ann-Marta know?

"And if I did?" the man challenged Fairchild abrasively. "The UN controls the galaxy, Fairchild. Michigan State operates under contracts we tender. You are an employee whose services could be terminated in an instant, if I demanded."

Teisha glanced at Ann-Marta, amazed that the woman was willing to let this go on. Didn't she understand how important all this was? How critical it would be to bring in an entirely new staff of linguists and sociologists to study the dragons?

Oh.

A whole, new staff. Replace absolutely everyone on the ground with UN staffers. Evict her and either destroy Paz's hexagon project or let it go entirely feral, because Teisha Montjoy and her experts would no longer be around to study.

Was that what this vulture was all about?

Teisha caught Fairchild's smile at the man. It looked remarkably like Teisha's mother had, listening to some fanciful yarn intended to cover up having forbidden cookies in one hand.

"No," Fairchild said simply.

And then ignored the man and went back to her noodles, cutting off bits for the dragons to sample, like they were in the process of doing from every plate where someone was offering some interesting delicacy. Even Ambassador Chaplin, since he was being polite to the natives.

As much of a shit as he was being to the humans.

"No?" the man demanded. "You have no leverage here, Fairchild."

"Oh, but I do," she smiled, almost goading the man in ways Teisha didn't realize her pilot had in her.

But nobody really knew that much about Fairchild, beyond the fame and fortune.

Nobody but Ann-Marta, it seemed.

What had happened on *Escudra VI* that never made the news?

"You will tell me this instant," Chaplin snapped, ratcheting things back up to the point that all three dragons were poised.

It did not look like they were intending to flee, either.

She wondered if Chaplin understood just how similar to dragons from *Earth*'s fantasy literature their little friends were. The video of that idiot eagle in flames hadn't made it to *Earth* yet.

"Governor Montjoy, under the Treaty of Cardiff," the woman drawled the syllables out slowly. Exquisitely, like drawing a razor blade over the flesh of a ripe tomato. "Ambassador Fairchild, under the Treaty of Cardiff."

"We can get that overridden, madame."

Chaplin's voice had grown cold and ugly. Teisha wondered if he understood that the dragons were preparing to defend her from the two males. And if anyone would help the man, at least other than making sure he got to a hospital bed quickly after it happened. Assuming he survived. Eagles didn't.

Teisha had developed a marked antipathy to the man in the last thirty seconds. Probably why Ann-Marta had distracted her.

What did that woman know?

"Normally, Ambassador Chaplin, this would be the point where I challenged you to give it your best shot," Fairchild smiled at the man. "To take it to the floor of the General Assembly and have it out in public. Or even in secret session of the Permanent Security Council. However, I think that would be counter-productive."

"Good, you are beginning to see reason, then?" Chaplin said, almost preening.

"No," Fairchild grinned. "I still think you are something of an asshole, Ambassador, but I am required to treat you with respect, as I am also an Ambassador here. At present, you can terminate my contract with MSU via either Doc Montjoy or the Provost, but I'll just go to work for my *other clients* at that point, so nothing at all will change."

Okay, so maybe Ann-Marta did know more than she was letting on. And Fairchild was far more than anyone had ever suggested. There were depths of knowledge and savvy that Teisha had not expected.

But then she remembered Eleanor, who had not spoken once during all this. AIs of that caliber were extremely expensive. That suggested that Fairchild came from money. Lots of it.

Her academic record had been second quintile, but her piloting credentials absolutely first class. Was that her secret? Teisha knew she just wanted to fly, and her fame meant that she could fly anywhere she really wanted, so she had taken another MSU contract. And done just fine, right up to the point she upended the galaxy a second time.

Chaplin started to say something, and Mathieu interrupted by placing a calming hand on the man's arm. Chaplin turned and something unsaid passed between the two men.

He nodded, then turned back to Fairchild.

"You are correct, Madame Ambassador," he said coldly. "We should not get caught up in personality as we seek to solve this situation. Perhaps we should finish our lunch and then take the rest of the day off, reconvening in the morning to discuss things."

"Thank you, Ambassador Chaplin," Fairchild said politely. "That would be lovely."

Teisha watched all the energy and emotion drain out of things. Everybody ate mechanically at that point except N'drn, who warbled and chirped like a gourmand who has found a new favorite restaurant.

What would tomorrow bring?

CHAPTER THIRTY-FIVE

R'WN

R'WN HAD NOT FOLLOWED the words at lunch, but the emotions were obvious. He suspected that many things had changed, but after a certain confrontation, everyone had gone silent and cold. Not hostile, but withdrawn some.

Now, they were in the room that smelled of Fairchild, down to an old sweatshirt dropped at the foot of the bed at some point and probably forgotten while she was camping in dragonland. M'nth had claimed it. N'drn was on a giant wooden building made of smaller containers that pulled out to reveal more clothing.

R'wn was on a chair watching Fairchild settle at the far end of the bed.

"Thank you," she said simply.

"For?" R'wn chirped back.

He watched those enormous arms come out and circle to include the entire nest. And all the people that he had met today, good and bad. But dragons were the same. Some were nice. Some were shits.

The key was always in identifying who were going to be

rude fuckers ahead of time so you could prepare for it. Like the two males from the stars.

He hopped over to the bed and climbed up on Fairchild's stomach, tapping one claw noisily against the tablet in her pouch.

She pulled it out and rested it where he could reach.

Doing it this way was a pain in the tail, but they were only slowly getting better at understanding each other. What he really needed was for someone to make a version of the magic slate that was dragon-sized. Or could listen to chirps and translate them into human. Eleanor had said she was working on such a magical artifact, but that it would take time.

Sub-boss fuckers? he scrawled and let her read it.

She laughed out loud, which was his intent. Fairchild needed to relax.

She swiped the question mark for an exclamation point and R'wn nodded in turn, laughing.

Also important +2, she added below that.

Ah, so just beneath Skygod Katou, back at the human nest. Most powerful and possibly dangerous, at least for personality.

The human would still ignite mightily if he was a threat to her or his friends.

Things might get ugly afterwards, but Fairchild would be safe.

"What are you grumbling about?" M'nth asked from the other end of the bed.

"How to protect Fairchild," he turned to her. "The new strangers are dangerous personalities, intent on being fuckers."

"Just be careful," she warned him. "They are as close to gods as we're ever going to meet. They might be able to wipe out all the dragons with a wave of their hand, if we pissed them off enough."

"Noted," R'wn said.

Just because, he climbed back up Fairchild again, curling up on her shoulder with his wing against her neck. She purred. It was good.

"So what should we do about allies?" N'drn asked now. "Montjoy and Ann-Marta seem friendly. Should I consult with the other professor and see where her loyalties lie?"

R'wn grabbed hold as Fairchild moved, but she was only reaching for the tablet.

He watched her draw a map, with his nest in one corner, the planet called *Biysk* according to the humans. In a different corner, she drew this human nest, with a line connecting to another nest that was the Michigan State University from which the powerful Spartan hieroglyph originated.

The last corner was the Union of Nests of the humans, spanning many worlds. Fairchild wrote Chp'ln's name there, while Jm'shdeh was attached to Michigan State directly.

So, four sides, all connected strangely, but at least he was sure of the players. He climbed down onto her keel and added Montjoy to the local human nest and Fairchild to his nest.

She made a noise he was unprepared for, and water seemed to be draining from her eyes in a strange way. Her breath had gone ragged as well.

Are hurt? he wrote quickly, prepared to bugle for someone to come.

Are fine, she wrote back quickly, still sniffly and leaking.

"She is overwhelmed by emotion, R'wn," Eleanor spoke up for the first time in many hours.

Fairchild leaned back now and he climbed up between

her breasts to talk to the friendly demon. M'nth joined him quickly.

"Overwhelmed?" he asked Eleanor, aware that she was gaining fluency in dragon daily.

"You accept her as friend and dragon," the demon explained patiently. "Fairchild has never truly belonged anywhere."

"Outcast?" M'nth asked.

"Adventurer," Eleanor replied, using the word that both N'drn and M'nth occasionally used to describe a certain botanist they knew.

M'nth climbed the rest of the way up and gave the human woman a kiss on the snout. R'wn did the same, and ended up holding claws with M'nth on Fairchild's chest. The breathing settled some.

It was good. She was a dragon. Those other punks would have to deal with him if they thought otherwise.

CHAPTER THIRTY-SIX

THE GOVERNOR of *Biysk* had settled in her office with a bottle of Japanese Scotch and two glasses. The sky was fast turning salmon-red out her window as the sun settled. Ann-Marta had gotten the prettyboys settled and handed off to some grad students this afternoon, for a tour of the base and the nearest hexagon.

Teisha had quietly made it clear to everyone involved that if they went anywhere near R'wn's nest she would fire the lot of them and then blackball them academically. Permanently. There were not many threats effective against students, but withholding letters of recommendation after they were on her project, and perhaps mentioning to prospective employers that she would never work with someone again, was high on that list.

Teisha poured as Ann-Marta settled.

"How bad is it?" she asked.

"They managed to load about half of the cargo on my list," Ann-Marta replied with a sigh. "And according to people on the ship that was only because the station crew worked overnight when the departure orders came down, else they would have barely had enough food for the ship's crew."

"Do we need to start rationing yet?" Teisha asked. "We have made some progress here, and can ramp up planting vegetables in controlled plots within the wire, but those will take a while to reach maturity."

"I would suggest you proceed anyway," Ann-Marta replied seriously. "At a minimum, it will keep some of the undergrads out of trouble."

"I might suggest they write up their findings and I'll give them lead investigator credit on papers, too," Teisha laughed. "That will motivate a great many of them."

Ann-Marta nodded, smiling a little, however grimly.

"We're still down considerably on what we should have for food stocks against an emergency," the woman said.

Teisha had an idea. A rude one. A terribly wicked touch of evil. Ann-Marta must had seen something in her face.

"Yes?" she drawled.

"So we need supplies and the UN basically hijacked my transport, right?" Teisha asked.

"I might not use the word *hijack* for legal reasons but essentially true."

"So I presumably need to send it home as quickly as you can get it unloaded and get everything down to the surface," Teisha noted. "That rather nicely puts our new friends on the spot, doesn't it?"

"How so?"

"They either have that long before they need to leave aboard *Beagle*, or they are stuck here until our ship returns a second time," Teisha said. "And *Beagle* is rather slow, compared to just about any other ship out there, so they might be stuck here a while."

"What if he announces that you have been removed as governor?" Ann-Marta asked.

"Then he has to feed everyone himself." Teisha felt her face grow hard. "Without sufficient food. Doubly so if the fucker carries through with his threat to fire me from the project, or shut the project down. It would take *Beagle* at least four trips just to evacuate all the gear and people we have on hand right now. Plus at that point he's getting into damage clauses with MSU and I can't imagine Emerson not going public in a loud and ugly way. The UN still isn't all that popular in the old United States, for reasons going back centuries."

"So we're going to play hardball?" Ann-Marta asked.

Teisha didn't figure it mattered all that much to the woman. Northmen Services would just move on to the next contract. If it wasn't with MSU, it might be Mexico City Polytechnic, or someone equally flush with funds.

"We'll prepare for him to push that hard," Teisha countered. "I'd rather he came, he saw, and he went home to file reports telling people about our strawberry dragons. We know so much more than we did before, just based on all the documentation Fairchild and Eleanor have written up for us since *Beagle* left, as well as folks meeting R'wn and his friends. That will help."

"And if he decides to push?"

"I have tenure. And I am the Governor of *Biysk* under the Treaty of Cardiff," Teisha replied coldly. "He's welcome to try."

CHAPTER THIRTY-SEVEN

FAIRCHILD

FAIRCHILD HAD SLEPT. On *Earth*, lizards tended to be cold-blooded, needing heat from the sun or the environment to warm up. Three dragons under the covers with her generated more heat than a German Shepherd, to the point she'd thrown the blanket off at one point and just had her T-shirt and sheet.

It helped that she was indoors and there was a heater blowing warm air around. She'd been in a hard-sided tent for nearly two months, sleeping rough.

She got up and headed for the shower, three dragons along with her, swooping and stalling. The communal was divided into three parts, where shy boys and girls could be off by themselves, but the majority of the heads were in a single room down both sides, and the place was starting to get busy. Early yet, but she'd been rising with the sun and that hadn't changed today.

Still, the room fell to silence when she walked in and stripped. Normally, all the attention would be nice, but nobody was staring at her bottom today. The three goofs got all the eyes.

Fairchild cranked the heat up to soak. R'wn tasted it and yelped at it being too hot, so she grabbed the next head over and put it to lukewarm. The humans freaked at the exchange, and then just stood there open-mouthed when all three dragons proceeded to rinse.

A shadow approached, causing Fairchild to look up.

Ambassador Chaplin. Nude, like her and everybody else.

Rail thin, like her, but even skinnier. Eight-pack of abs, so he must work at that muscle tone. Taller than her by a hand or so. Pretty, but she'd done prettier. And homelier. And just about everything in between.

"Good morning," he said carefully, aware that everyone was naked in here and the dragons still had claws.

"Heya," Fairchild replied.

Not much to say, and probably not the place for it, with so many witnesses, so she went back to scrubbing her hair.

"They seem to be enjoying themselves," Chaplin said over the noise of the water.

"This is their first shower," Fairchild replied ambiguously. "I've been in the field, so this is only my third in something like six weeks, not counting cold dips in the pond."

"So you have been truly living in the bush?" he asked, getting his water set just right before stepping into it.

And possibly ogling her a bit as he did. Fairchild didn't mind.

"Only way to learn," she replied. "To understand. They have a pretty sophisticated society, but some of the things they think and do are so alien that it doesn't make any sense. And they seem extremely advanced for the primitive state of their technology, but I'm wondering if being able to fly and breathe fire means that they are not the barely-Bronze age primitives people think."

"What are they, then?" he asked, turned to her.

Fairchild got the soap out of her hair and maybe

stretched herself invitingly a little to distract the man, enjoying the physical attention after so long utterly celibate.

"Dragons," she shrugged. "I am not a sociologist, but nobody else on this planet was, either, so I got promoted by the Governor."

Always remind the man that they went to the Treaty of Cardiff to handle things. Official and legal, as it were.

He washed his hair. It was wavy and so dark dry that it almost looked black. She could see grays coming in underneath, kind of like hers, but his was a helmet and hers was going to stripe in weird ways, like an interstellar zebra.

"Cardiff has certain implications," Chaplin said, not raising his voice so much as focusing it entirely on her.

The others in here had seemed intent on ignoring this whole scene and getting gone quickly. Not counting three extremely alert dragons.

"I am aware of that, Ambassador," Fairchild replied firmly. "Dr. Montjoy reviewed everything with her staff for several days before making that declaration. And unless you brought new treaties, nothing the UN has done has formed a better way to keep things stable while humans figure out what they want to do."

"Why not the dragons?" he asked.

"They are only barely beginning to grasp the implications, Ambassador," she said. "R'wn mistook me for a god at first, and then a demon hunting him for the crime of trespassing on holy ground. It was only later that he decided I was as big a dork as him."

"What do you want out of all this, Fairchild?" he asked.

Ah, the ten million loonie question. What is the famous Fairchild up to?

Clean, she shut down her water and then the dragons' as well. They were just goofing around in the spray anyway.

"I want to fly, Chaplin," she said, staring at the man and daring him to say anything.

When he didn't, she nodded and chirped at the others, heading for her towel and clean clothes.

Chaplin eventually caught up with her in the dining hall, arriving just after her and being three places back in the sparse food line. Fairchild wasn't fooled. She could smell a social ambush a kilometer away.

Her tray had two plates, one for her and one for the gang, filled with their various favorites gleaned from six weeks of trying what she ate.

And coffee. None of the dragons drank it, which was just fine with her. Less to share around.

Chaplin ended up across the table from her, but it wasn't a confrontation.

As long as nobody called it a date.

He was, of course, eating the most healthy things possible this morning. Egg whites, fruit, wheat toast. Fool didn't have any gravy anywhere.

For all her slim figure, Fairchild knew she was a hummingbird, constantly burning calories to the point that if she didn't get enough with breakfast then lethargy would set in by lunch.

Today, that included gravy. Over just about everything.

The man across from her was cute. But partly that was the way he was aging into his face a little. The other one was just too damned pretty. And he hadn't said anything about the various ink drawings on her flesh, which he'd now seen all of.

Fairchild could cover everything with sleeves and pants, as long as she planned her wardrobe for maximum effect. Paella had been the expert there, teaching her the finer details.

"So what are we going to argue about today?" she asked innocently as three dragons munched and chirped.

She noted that every one of them was seated with the Ambassador in front of them, in case they needed to blast him. Fairchild didn't think it would be necessary, but they were protecting her. They had accepted her.

She had a tribe.

It was still weird, *belonging*. She'd never done that. But then, Rudy was eight years older than her and Eva twenty, so they had all been grown-up and largely gone by the time she was conscious enough to understand what was going on.

Various shrinks and counselors had worked with her on abandonment issues. Eleanor had always been there for her, even when little Lady Dani had left her places, either accidentally or on purpose. But she was programmed that way, so she really didn't have a choice.

The dragons had chosen her. Adopted her. Were willing to flame a pissy eagle across a breakfast table for her, if necessary.

Tears wanted to well up and she forced them to remain invisible. Yet another useful skill one developed around Alphonse Cooper, Sr.'s household.

"We are not going to argue," he said simply. "Discuss, perhaps. But I was sent here with certain instructions and the power to implement them."

"So you'll just roll over everyone else?" Fairchild challenged him.

"We will do this my way, Ambassador Fairchild," he answered in a hard voice.

"It is their planet," she reminded him. "Not even the SecGen can simply wish that away. If you intend to make changes, those have to be had out in the General Assembly. I have been studying law for the last several weeks."

"They cannot be allowed to stand in the way of progress," the man almost snarled at her.

"Why not?" Fairchild fired back. "There are dozens if not hundreds of other worlds that we've discovered. Hell, the fact that they are all so perfect for humans is why the boffins assumed that the Elder Race existed, to have made it so."

"And you are an expert on them?" he sneered.

"I found the first tangible evidence that all those theories weren't pure hokum, Chaplin," she smiled. "Accidentally, true, but I've swam in those waters, literally as well as figuratively. There are other places we can go. If you destroy *Biysk*, you've ended all chance for another intelligent, tool-using species to develop."

"And if they become a threat to humans?"

Fairchild couldn't help the laughter that erupted out of her mouth. It was almost as cathartic as last night's cry. For different reasons, though.

She lowered a hand, palm up.

"R'wn?" she chirped. "Would you?"

R'wn looked up from his hunk of sausage patty and studied things. She was smiling. Chaplin was scowling even more than usual, but a little confused now, like he'd been sandbagged.

R'wn hopped up on her hand with a cheery whistle that she didn't translate.

"What are we going to do to this fucker?" wasn't the sort of thing you explained to a visiting Ambassador.

She held her hand out so that R'wn was face-level with Chaplin. They studied each other for a long second.

"How, exactly, do you think a strawberry dragon is a threat to humanity?" she asked simply. "There are more humans on this base than dragons in his nest, if I did the math right. And nests are not that common, because each requires a certain territory to hunt and harvest from. I suspect that Paris alone has more humans than there are dragons combined, because they don't really do heat or cold extremes. We have not, however, done a rigorous survey of other climates to date, so I could be wrong there."

Fairchild lowered her hand.

"Thank you, R'wn," she said.

He chirped happily and went back to his breakfast.

"M'nth would really like to know how to work iron, Chaplin," she continued. "You know, steel tools about the size of one of our teeth. We have several thousand years head start, so if they are suddenly going to overwhelm us technologically, I expect that we'd actually deserve it at that point."

She reached for her coffee and watched the man. He ate mechanically and studied her back, but it wasn't a hottie across the bar checking her out. Nor was it a mugger measuring her for a punch.

But at the end of the day, she'd been recording everything. Well, Eleanor had, for her. Fairchild could prove that she'd been trying to be reasonable at every step. In the court of public opinion if nothing else.

Might not hold water with UN bureaucrats, but she'd happily release everything to the press and let them have a feeding frenzy. Maybe ask one of Father's attorneys to chum the water for her, even.

"There are larger concerns than you and your dragons, Fairchild," he finally said. "The UN had already declared this experiment a success and was in the process of allocating colonial grants."

"Ah, so you've sold your soul for money," she nodded sagely. Dismissively.

We all finally give up on our dreams and settle, don't we?

Except that she hadn't. Couldn't. Wasn't how she was wired.

How many times had Father cut off her credit over the years because she wouldn't settle down and marry someone that would make a good business partnership? Or forbade her from this or that, because he thought that she hadn't inherited stubborn from either side of the family?

The man turned red. Then white. Probably rage, from the way his pupils dilated.

She held a coffee mug just exactly as one would when they were preparing to throw it in someone's face. Not that she'd ever gotten out of a mugging that way. Or an attempted rape.

"Not all of us are born extravagantly wealthy, Lady Cooper," he finally said quietly.

Ah, so you dug deep enough, did you? Think you've found the truth? Found Alphonse Cooper, Sr. and think that gives you leverage over me?

Fairchild wondered if she should send Father a message directly, telling him that the UN was prying into his personal business affairs.

That might cause a man like him to overthrow entire governments, knowing Father's rage. Might be all sorts of fun to watch.

But she had a lever on Chaplin now. One he had handed her himself.

"Did you know that when I changed my name, he changed his will?" she asked. "Five way split among his children went to four? I'll get nothing at all from the Cooper estate. He thought that would punish me into complying with his demands."

"Did it?" Chaplin asked in a sour tone.

"No, it freed me," Fairchild replied with a smile. "He lost the last hold he might have had. Once I learned how to fly, it was the only thing I ever wanted to do. And I will, as long as I can. I took this job because it put me in a wingsuit regularly and let me see the universe. There are things money simply cannot buy."

"So you cannot be bought?" Chaplin asked. "Is that what you are telling me?"

"I doubt you have the right coin anyway," she said, careful not to sound snotty or condescending. "I have to protect my friends, at least until they understand enough about how things work to handle the job themselves. I'm looking forward to the first dragon that passes the bar exam and is licensed to practice law in New York State. Talk about fun."

"Fun?" Chaplin asked, confused.

"You don't see them as people, Chaplin," she said. "To you, they appear to be animals, however well trained, or a problem to be solved. That's like deciding that Shanghai is a *problem that must be solved*."

"And your proposal negatively impacts a tremendous number of people, Fairchild," he said. "But you didn't give any care to that, did you?"

She drank coffee rather than react. Paella always reminded her to measure your victim twice before cutting him to pieces.

"You know, I would have to look up the various statutes to be absolutely certain," Fairchild mused. "However, I am pretty certain that if you are personally invested in a company with a potential colonial grant on the line, your mere presence here as an Ambassador and representative of Secretary General Katou is extremely unethical. Probably illegal in most jurisdictions as well, considering the basis for conflict of interest inherent. Does he know? Does anybody in a position of authority? Mind you, I've had to study a lot of interstellar law the last two months."

His eyes got big. Nervous.

Fairchild smiled. It was a predatory smile. The result of

way too much adulting lately. Actually reading law books and crap like that while the dragons were busy playing or working or sleeping.

You want to fight this in the court of public opinion, princess? Let me see you survive that shark feeding frenzy, if any whiff of that comes out.

At least she'd taken the time to fly two patrols each day, rain or shine, just so she had skytime as well as adulting time.

Woman spends that much time alone learns to think, in spite of herself.

Before anyone said anything more, Chaplin's eyes locked on something over her left shoulder and he flexed his entire body downwards. The dragons got a little chirpy but nobody screamed *Eagle!* yet.

"We will discuss this again at a later time," he said quietly.

Whether that was a threat or a promise was left unsaid. Lousy foreplay, unless he was into that sort of personal, emotional abuse. She'd known a few folks like that.

Teisha Montjoy slipped into the chair on her left. Ann-Marta took the one on her right.

"Good news," Doc announced in a quiet voice.

"Oh?" Chaplin asked in a completely different tone than ten seconds ago.

She must have been getting to the man, because this was what he sounded like with all emotions removed from his voice.

"The transport *Columbia* just arrived in-system and signaled," Montjoy said.

Fairchild understood the reference, but Chaplin was completely lost.

"That vessel belongs to Paz Hernandez," Fairchild offered to the man helpfully. "The woman who largely funded this project in the early days. And who continues to be our biggest backer."

He blinked at her, but the man was still finding his footing after nearly falling off a ledge.

At least she hadn't pushed him.

Yet.

Fairchild smiled knowingly. *Measure twice.*

"Oh, and in addition to Paz, she apparently has several guests aboard," Teisha added, her own voice suddenly like gooey frosting on a cupcake. "Secretary General Katou, among others."

Oh, shit. Skygod was here?

Fairchild grabbed her tablet and quickly scrawled a note for the gang. They needed to know. To plan.

You handle, R'wn scrawled back and Fairchild was nearly crying again.

Her take charge of dealing with the Secretary General of the United Nations for the dragons?

Shit. That was about as adulting as it got.

"Oh, and Fairchild, the note said to specifically tell you that Alphonse Cooper was aboard, as well," Doc said.

She turned to look at the woman. Then the other direction to get confirmation from Ann-Marta. Teisha didn't know, but Ann-Marta did. She nodded.

"So it's out of our hands now," Fairchild told Chaplin.

"What did R'wn say to you just now that was so important?" he asked.

Shit, had he been watching her that closely, to see the little flinch?

Fairchild drew a hard breath.

"He reiterated that I was the Ambassador to the Dragons, Ambassador Chaplin," she said simply. "That he expected me to handle those negotiations, at least until it was time to bring in the nest elders."

"You will do an exceptional job, Fairchild," he said.

She blinked back tears, then let them come.

Right now, she was surrounded by friends, and even Chaplin had maybe decided not to be an enemy. Man must not have suicidal tendencies.

Fairchild understood those. She'd lost track of how many times those thoughts had taken her right up to the edge. A few more grams of pressure on a trigger. A handful of extra pills in the wrong combination.

Make it all go away.

But then she would never get to fly again. That had been the price she'd never been willing to pay.

M'nth waddled over, tapped her hand, and then climbed right up her arm when she held it still. R'wn's sort-of girlfriend kissed her on the cheek, like she had taken to doing. Like maybe she understood.

Maybe they did.

Because they loved her. Accepted her.

Trusted her.

She could do this thing.

FAIRCHILD WATCHED the shuttle settle on the landing pad. The setting sun behind it almost made the image something she'd want to hang on a wall somewhere. If she ever had walls. It had come down with the sort of delicacy not many pilots could manage. Her on a good day, but only the good ones.

But then, Paz Hernandez had the sort of money to hire the best. And this shuttle, while it was a workhorse, a *Qunsahr Industries Shuttle, Mark 4, Heavy*, it was still painted elegantly, although a mural of Mexican history down the side looked a little weird to her eye.

Fairchild was standing at the center of the little group, with R'wn on her shoulder, since they together represented First Contact. N'drn was with Teisha and M'nth rode on Ann-Marta. Ambassador Chaplin and his sidekick were next to Fairchild on her left, with Dr. Jamshidi on the outside.

Chaplin had actually turned into a nice enough guy in the last two days, as *Columbia* slid down into orbit and then deployed the big lander. Most likely didn't want to provoke someone like Fairchild into spilling all his private business to the news organizations before he had a chance to do some damage control first.

Teisha and Ann-Marta had also been overjoyed at the news, when they found out that Paz had loaded up her personal ship with supplies and dragged several people along.

Three figures walked down the ramp as Fairchild led people over on foot.

Paz was in the middle, which was weird, considering the combined power and wealth of the two men with her. She was tiny. Barely over a meter and a half tall, and so slim that it looked like a stiff breeze could carry her away.

But one look at her face told you that it better be a hurricane with an attitude problem to even try. The woman was in her seventies. White hair shoulder length, and lots of wrinkles, like your favorite Mexican grandma.

On her left was UN Secretary General Vlasta Eduard Katou. Tall and heavy-set. Croat/Japanese, and one of the most powerful figures in the galaxy, right up there with the Pope and a few national leaders.

But it was the man on Paz's right that drew Fairchild's eye.

Almost as tall as Katou, but barely half the man's mass. Built rather like Fairchild, or maybe a heavier version of Ambassador Chaplin. Not as nice. Thousands of times wealthier.

Introductions went quickly, although she had to explain the meaning of the dragon vocalization for Skygod and the implications. Katou smiled and laughed at that.

Paz smiled up at her. It was a dangerous smile.

"So the messages were a bit confused," she began. "But I understood that *Beagle* had left *Earth* without its full cargo load because they were in a hurry."

Paz scowled at Chaplin, who had the courtesy to look pained and bow to the woman.

"Rather than risk my investment, I brought more," Paz continued. "And because I needed to investigate the current situation personally, I brought the Secretary General with me. And another of my new investors."

Fairchild blinked, but gave no other outward reaction. Father had invested in this project? Recently?

How recently? Perhaps after his estranged youngest daughter started working here as a contract pilot?

His serene smile when she looked suggested that, but she might never get the truth out of the man.

Not Alphonse Cooper.

And Paz had not outed her as the *former* Lady Danielle Cooper, daughter of said Alphonse, though it was probably an open secret with most of the people around her by now.

"Welcome to *Biysk*," Fairchild said simply.

"Greetings, skygod and friends," R'wn added a moment later, which she had to translate.

R'wn chirped at her and held out a hand, so Fairchild did. The dragon climbed down her arm and got closer to the skygod, without flying around. He understood how nervous some people got, at least at first.

Vlasta Katou bent down to study the dragon. R'wn studied the man.

A moment later, R'wn turned to her and smiled.

"Not a fucker," he announced in dragon, causing her, Eleanor, N'drn, and M'nth to snort.

"What was that?" Katou asked.

"R'wn has decided that he likes you, sir," Fairchild said carefully, leaving out all the context.

R'wn had even revised his opinion of Chaplin some, but that was mostly the man behaving better, now that he knew he'd been shunted to one side by circumstances beyond his control.

Ann-Marta got everyone loaded into ground vehicles as

her staff and every available student started unloading the Mark 4. Small talk got them to the administration building, and the staff had laid on a big dinner, using precious supplies once they knew that there was a whole second ship in orbit with food.

They were at a table set up for visiting dignitaries, although nothing like this had ever happened.

But then, this was the first time humans had met their peers in fifty thousand years.

Dinner was not embarrassing for anyone. The dragons had prepared by having her fly them to the nest to pick up various foodstuffs to trade for what she had brought. No nest elders had come, but they had wanted the crazy dragons to deal with the outsiders first, anyway.

Fairchild figured they would come around, once they finally understood that the universe beyond the trees was here to stay.

After dinner, Fairchild somehow wasn't surprised to find herself alone as people had a larger cocktail party with ground staff and academics. It was the first party in a while, but not the last. More people would be coming, but Governor Montjoy would be in charge of sorting it all out.

So when Alphonse wandered into her corner, R'wn chirped a greeting and Fairchild held up her glass of Scotch in toast. He clinked his own glass against it and walked close enough that the three of them could have a quiet conversation. Four, actually, except that Eleanor would not speak to her father unless ordered.

She rather disliked the man, but it was entirely personal. At least as personal as an artificially intelligent computer program could make it. Not that Fairchild argued with her logic.

"So what brings you to *Biysk*?" she asked carefully, aware of the sometimes volcanic nature of her father's temper. And she didn't call him *Father* in public these days. He had cut her off.

"I've known Paz for thirty years," he replied, just as carefully. "Her coming, and doing it so loudly that she shamed the UN into action, gave me an excuse."

Fairchild nodded. She'd never gotten the plain truth out of the man.

Never once.

"And I wanted to see the situation for myself," Alphonse continued unprompted. "See what these people would make of it, but more importantly, to see how you handled it."

"I've done as well as I could, with a variety of advisors and a lot of experience," Fairchild found herself saying defensively.

"You've done better than that, Fairchild," he said, calling her by her chosen name, instead of *Dani*. Small wins? "You've taken an impossible situation, and boiled it down into clear, understandable terms. In the last two days I have read a number of the reports you filed. Those were exceptionally well done."

Fairchild felt herself blush. R'wn felt it too, because he leaned in and rubbed a wing against her neck to comfort her.

"So what is the UN going to do?" she asked.

He might not be involved, but the man had just spent time trapped on a transport with the skygod and Paz Hernandez. The topic would have come up, especially as *Columbia* had almost caught up with the slower *Beagle* getting here.

"Their hands are tied," Alphonse said with a wicked grin now. "Paz will see to that, as she wants the entire planet turned into something of a national park for the dragons. The woman was utterly taken with the idea, even before N'drn charmed her so well over dinner."

"He can be a bit of a showman, given the chance," Fairchild noted.

"Precisely," her father agreed. "The dragons change everything. Paz will make even more money from it. So will I, since I invested at exactly the right time, as shares had been at a ten-year-low with the troubles that caused the old services company to be fired."

"Is that all?" she asked.

Fairchild couldn't help the shade of hurt in her voice, but eighty-seven-year-old Alphonse and thirty-three-year-old Dani had never seen eye to eye on just about anything.

"No," Alphonse replied, his own voice a little husky. "I wanted to see my youngest daughter, and tell her how proud I was of her."

Fairchild—the former Lady Danielle Cooper—let the tears come as her Father wrapped his free hand around her shoulders. It was almost as good as a dragon's kiss for what ailed her.

Blaze Ward writes science fiction in the Alexandria Station universe (Jessica Keller, The Science Officer, The Story Road, etc.) as well as several other science fiction universes, such as Star Dragon, the Dominion, and more. He also writes odd bits of high fantasy with swords and orcs. In addition, he is the Editor and Publisher of *Boundary Shock Quarterly Magazine*. You can find out more at his website www.blazeward.com, as well as Facebook, Goodreads, and other places.

Blaze's works are available as ebooks, paper, and audio, and can be found at a variety of online vendors. His newsletter comes out regularly, and you can also follow his blog on his website. He really enjoys interacting with fans, and looks forward to any and all questions—even ones about his books!

Never miss a release!
If you'd like to be notified of new releases, sign up for my newsletter.

http://www.blazeward.com/newsletter/

Buy More!
Did you know that you can buy directly from my website?

https://www.blazeward.com/shop/

ABOUT KNOTTED ROAD PRESS

Knotted Road Press fiction specializes in dynamic writing set in mysterious, exotic locations.

Knotted Road Press non–fiction publishes autobiographies, business books, cookbooks, and how–to books with unique voices.

Knotted Road Press creates DRM–free ebooks as well as high–quality print books for readers around the world.

With authors in a variety of genres including literary, poetry, mystery, fantasy, and science fiction, Knotted Road Press has something for everyone.

Knotted Road Press
www.KnottedRoadPress.com